PUFFIN BOOKS

BLACK JACK

Young Bartholomew Dorking stood in the dark, quiet room and looked down at the coffin and the huge ruffian, lately taken down from the gallows, who lay there, seemingly carved out of stone. Suddenly he noticed that the eyes were open and staring at him with a dreadful entreaty. The villain was alive! And that was how the gentle young apprentice came to find his life entangled with a murdering villain, forced to help him for fear of the dreadful crimes he would commit if he were let loose on the world.

This is a wild story which takes its astonishing violent way through the seamiest parts of London, a travelling circus and a private madhouse where forgotten lunatics are chained in empty rooms and from which young Tolly rescues Belle, the girl who isn't really mad at all.

It is recommended for readers with strong nerves and a taste for melodrama.

An older Puffin for readers of eleven and over.

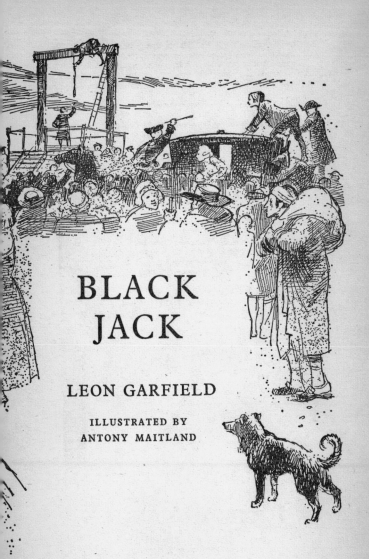

BLACK JACK

LEON GARFIELD

ILLUSTRATED BY
ANTONY MAITLAND

PUFFIN BOOKS

Puffin Books, Penguin Books Ltd, Harmondsworth, Middlesex, England
Penguin Books, 40 West 23rd Street, New York, New York 10010, U.S.A.
Penguin Books Australia Ltd, Ringwood, Victoria, Australia
Penguin Books Canada Ltd, 2801 John Street, Markham, Ontario, Canada L3R 1B4
Penguin Books (N.Z.) Ltd, 182–190 Wairau Road, Auckland 10, New Zealand

—

First published by Longmans Young Books 1968
Published in Penguin Books 1971
Reprinted 1972, 1973, 1974, 1976, 1977, 1978, 1979, 1980,
1983, 1984

—

—

Made and printed in Great Britain
by Richard Clay (The Chaucer Press) Ltd,
Bungay, Suffolk
Set in Linotype Plantin

For Grace Hogarth

THERE are many queer ways of earning a living; but none so quaint as Mrs Gorgandy's. She was a Tyburn widow. Early and black on a Monday morning, she was up at the Tree, all in a tragical flutter, waiting to be bereaved.

Sometimes, it's true, she was forestalled by a wife or mother; then Mrs Gorgandy curtsied and withdrew – not wanting to come between flesh and flesh.

But, in general, she knew her business and picked on those that were alone in the world – the real villainous outcasts such as everyone was glad to see hanged – to stand wife or mother to in their last lonely moments. And even after.

It was the *after* that mattered. Many and many were the unloved ones weeping Mrs Gorgandy had begged strangers to help her cut down as they ticked and tocked in the diabolical geometry of the gallows.

'Oh, sir! The good God'll reward you for your kindness to a mint-new widder! Ah! Careful with 'im, sir! For though 'e's dead as mutton, mortal flesh must be respected! Here's 'is box! Mister Ketch!' (To the hangman.) 'Mister Ketch, love – a shilling if you goes past me house with the remains. Seven Blackfriars Lane, love.'

Then, her sad merchandise aboard, Mrs Gorgandy would lift up her skirts and, with a twitter of violet stockings, join her 'late loved one' on his last journey but one.

His last journey of all would not yet have been fixed on; Mrs Gorgandy had yet to settle with any surgeon who'd pay upwards of seven pound ten for a corpse in good condition.

And so to the hanging of Black Jack on Monday, April fourteen, 1749.

A vast ruffian, nearly seven foot high and broad to match,

who'd terrorized the lanes about Knightsbridge till a quart of rum and five peace officers had laid him low.

'Poor soul!' had sighed Mrs Gorgandy when she'd learned of Black Jack's coming cancellation. 'When there's breath in you, you ain't worth two penn'orth of cold gin; yet your mint-new widder might fairly ask fifteen pound ten for your remainders. And get it, too!'

She must have been at the Tree all night, for first comers saw her already propping up a gallows' post against the rising sun like a great black slug.

'It's me 'usband, kind sir! Wicked, shocking sinner that 'e's been! But me dooty's 'ere to see 'im off and decently bestowed. Will you 'elp a poor widder-to-be, dear sir? For 'e's that 'eavy, 'e'd squash me flat! Oo'll 'elp? Oo'll 'elp?'

So she went on while round about her the crowd grew, and soon her sobby voice, though never stilled, was lost in the general hubbub of Tyburn Monday.

Who heard it? Did monstrous, scowling Black Jack when he came, swaying and rocking in the cart, with the parson on one side, praying for his soul, and the hangman on the other, praying for the rope which he dreaded would snap? For Black Jack was indeed a mighty fellow, and rough ... as if the Almighty had sketched him out (and left the Devil to fill him in) before He'd settled on something of a quieter, more genteel size.

'Oh, me sinful 'usband!' bawled Mrs Gorgandy. 'Look at 'im, kind sirs! Take pity and 'elp me with 'im when it's over! Oh, Jack, Jack! Bye-bye, me 'uge darling! May your going be easy, dear! Oh, sirs – I can't bear to watch! Cruel Mister Ketch is a-widdering me before me very eyes!'

She kept up her lamentations right till the moment Black Jack stepped off his launching-place, as if he'd been to Eternity born. Then she gave a loud shriek that wrung the hearts of all who didn't know her (country folk and suchlike who'd come up for the day) and entirely believed her to've been the perished ruffian's wife. Black Jack's great weight had come to his

aid and finished him off with a promptness most commend-
able.

With the widow aboard and the hangman at the helm, the
cart rocked away down Oxford Street, while a sea of heads
bobbed up beside it for a last peep into the open coffin – from
which they fell back, aghast and amazed ... Then the streets
grew narrower and narrower, choking off the chief of the
crowd till there were scarce fifty inquisitive souls remaining to
see the shipping of the coffin into Mrs Gorgandy's dark narrow
house – which looked like a coffin itself, with, maybe, another
house dead inside it.

But now there was a quickening of interest. Though they'd
turned him off as neat as kiss-your-hand, to lift Black Jack off
the cart was a task beyond the strength of the hangman and his
assistant. Desperately, they sweated and struggled. To no purpose. The crowd pressed forward, wondering if there might be
an upset. Mrs Gorgandy grew alarmed.

'Careful, Mister Ketch, love. Easy does it! Kind sirs, won't
nobody 'elp a mint-new widder? Don't nobody's 'eart bleed
for her?'

Shrewdly, her beady eyes flickered from face to face ...
then suddenly they twinkled.

'You, young sir – you got a nice, kind, rosy face ... like a
bowl of Kent cherries! Country-bred and country strong, I'll
take my oath! Come, dear, lend a hand and 'elp a poor widder
shift her grief and sorrow into 'er bereaved 'ome. And – and
'ere's a shilling for your kind 'eart!'

She'd fastened on a young apprentice, an agreeable, simple,
kindly-looking lad between fourteen and fifteen, whose cherry
complexion was provoked more by blushing at being picked
out of a crowd than by any country air he'd left behind. As
Mrs Gorgandy lived and breathed, not a lad to say 'no' even
without the shilling she'd pressed into his surprised hand.

Bartholomew Dorking, who'd been carried along on the
froth of the crowd, wished himself anywhere else in the world.

11

Even back in the draper's shop on Ludgate Hill where he was in the first month of his indentures. For he was of that age when public notice is as unwelcome as a fire at sea.

Awkwardly, and with sunsets in his cheeks, he went to the aid of the mint-new widow, morbidly afraid, the while, that he'd disgrace himself and let the burden fall. The hangman and his assistant stared down at him. Then they nodded and spat on their hands. Bartholomew bowed his head and braced his shoulders.

'Take the strain!'

Bartholomew took it. It nearly did for him. He staggered, tottered, all but fell. Mrs Gorgandy poked her frantic head down to see how he did.

'There's strength for you! There's power for you! There's determination for you! There's a kind heart for you! Two steps up, young sir. Take 'em easy. There's muscle for you! There's sturdiness for you! Just along this passage, young sir. Mind the banister! Nearly there ... in the parlour ... There's steadiness for you! There's manliness for you! And there's another shilling for you, dear!'

This last as the straining cortège entered the parlour at the end of the passage.

'On the table, gents –'

With a thump that shook the house the coffin was laid on a long scabbed table which, with a single wooden chair, was the only furnishing of the parlour.

Now, as Bartholomew Dorking leaned up against a wall to recover himself, came the law's last mortification of Black Jack. In accordance with the rewards of his office, the hangman deprived the dead man of his upper clothes; but Black Jack's small clothes were, alas, too patched and poor for even Mr Ketch's possessing.

During this ceremony Mrs Gorgandy hid her face in her hands and Bartholomew Dorking forgot his aching arms and torn new coat in grief and shame on the widow's behalf. But it was over quickly and tolerably respectfully: Black Jack, even in shabby, tumbled death was a formidable figure ... His shirt came up in great, capacious folds – like the foresail of a ship at the breaker's yard, to be stowed in a neat bundle under the hangman's arm.

'We've done, now, Mrs G.'

The widow looked up, smiled wanly, then offered gin to all concerned. But Mr Ketch and his assistant were already through the door. Bartholomew would have followed, but –

'Ah me kind young gent! Do a poor widder one more good turn on account of your dear warm 'eart!'

His way was blocked. The portly widow stood between him and escape. Faintly from the street he heard the ragged cheer and the jingle of harness as the hangman mounted up on his cart and rattled off. Though it was scarce midday, he had a curious feeling that night had just fallen and he was alone in it. Mrs Gorgandy smiled at him with mournful encouragement.

'One more good turn, young sir?'

He struggled not to look dismayed.

'Be glad to, ma'am.'

She sighed. 'Then just stay with 'im for 'alf an hour while I goes to – to gather 'is kith and kin to say a prayer and drink 'is – um – 'ealth before 'e goes to 'is last rest. I wouldn't ask dear, only some of 'em might call while I'm out and be fussed to get no answer. So if anyone knocks, just you say I'll be back directly and that the whopper's – um – poor Jack's safe and sound. 'Alf an hour, dear –'

She was mortally afraid she'd miss an important customer while she was out whistling up others. Then before he could answer, 'Gobblesshoo for your kind 'eart,' she sobbed – and slammed the door in the apprentice's startled face. The key turned in the lock and Mrs Gorgandy's footsteps pattered briskly over bare boards and out into the distant street. As if from another world, he heard her hoarse promise repeated: 'Back in 'alf an hour ...'

After a few moments he tried the door. The lock was secure. He went to the window – and discovered its cataract of dirt, dust and perished insects obscured three iron bars. Gloomily he wrote, 'Help. I am a prisoner,' with his finger on the cracked glass. Then he wrote it backwards in the hope someone in the strange country of the backs of houses and their secret yards might read it and come to his aid.

He went to the fireplace, in which there was a pile of ashes – as if a large family had burned their secrets there before going upstairs to hang themselves in a group. He looked up, and discovered the chimney to be partially blocked by a fall of bricks, two of which so resembled the soles of boots that Dorking wondered if some previous apprentice had tried to escape that way and failed.

He shivered – and reproached himself for thinking ill of the widow. The poor woman was half out of her mind with grief – and here was he thinking of nought but himself.

For shame, Bartholomew Dorking! Can you not spare half an hour out of your young life to sit decently and respectfully by a lonely coffin while the widow goes on her rounds? For shame, Bartholomew Dorking! Ain't she suffered this day without additions?

He sighed and sat in the solitary chair. It faced the window. Unhappy circumstance. Out of the end of the coffin poked Black Jack's great feet, rising up like cruel rocks exposed by a receded tide.

He turned the chair so that he might look at something more cheerful. Not that a dead man frightened him much. He came from Shoreham and drowned men washed up on the beach with the sea's general air of 'Is this yours? I don't want it', had made him familiar enough with corpses of all sizes and conditions. Even his father and mother had perished by the sea's endeavours and left him, early, to the command of a sea-captain uncle who had apprenticed him to the draper in Ludgate Hill rather than expose him to the orphaning ocean. ('Your soft heart, my boy, won't keep you afloat a moment.')

Dead men were sad sights, and Black Jack was no exception. Uneasily Bartholomew peered over his shoulder at the coffin. He half rose and stared, with the utmost respect, at the dead man's rocky face that lurked in a small forest of stiff black hair. It was not particularly peaceful. There was still a dismayed sort of scowl upon it, as if his soul had popped back to tell him that, when he'd jumped, it had been from the frypan into the fire.

He had returned to staring into the fireplace when he heard a far-off clock strike twice. The widow's half hour had lengthened. Dorking had an unpleasant thought that, distracted with grief, she'd forgotten him and plummetted into the river. He began to have thoughts of roaring for help and hurling himself at the door, when familiar footsteps pattered along the passage and a familiar voice called out: 'Anybody been, dear?'

'No, ma'am – not a soul –'

'There's a good boy. You'll find remains of a veal pie in the cupboard. Make yourself at 'ome. Back in 'alf an hour . . .'

Before he could protest she was off again, and 'Back in 'alf an hour' echoed from the street.

With the best will in the world, he was not equal to making himself at home. Even without the coffin, the room had a tomblike air and a remarkably musty smell. The remains of the veal pie, which was laid out on a low shelf in a cupboard facing the fireplace, looked unnaturally still – as if by 'remains', Mrs Gorgandy had had a deeper meaning . . .

Dorking shut the cupboard and, with a passing glance into the coffin (as if it was part of his duty to see that the dead man stayed where he was), went back to his chair by the fireplace.

To pass the time he fell to composing a letter to his uncle, the sea-captain, describing his adventure with all the wry humour of one who had been sent to London for a placid life.

Suddenly there were heavy footsteps in the passage. Came a knock on the door and a high, Scottish voice asking: 'Mrs Gorgandy? Are ye there, ma'am?'

'She'll be back in half an hour, sir. Who shall I say called?'

'Are ye – alone, boy?'

'Just me and Black Jack, sir.'

'Good – good. I'll be back. Tell her Hunter called. Don't forget. Doctor Hunter.'

'I'll tell her, sir. What time is it?'

'Quarter after four, laddie.'

The footsteps departed, leaving Bartholomew in a state of alarm that Mrs Gorgandy wouldn't return till nightfall and he'd be shut out of his master's shop till morning.

Indeed, as he stared to the grimy window, he saw the day outside already faltering and growing sullen, as if worn out with the effort of creeping into the room.

At half after six, a Dr Skimpole called.

'She'll be back in half an hour!' shouted Bartholomew desperately. 'Don't go off, sir! Please!'

'Don't worry, boy! I'll be back. Just you tell the lady to hold her fire till I return.'

'When will that be, sir?'

'The usual time, boy. Ten o'clock.'

With that the second doctor departed and the imprisoned boy's spirits suffered a further setback. Was he to be held in this dark, smelly and fearful room till ten? His master's shop was locked at seven: the family went to bed at nine ...

He banged on the door and shouted 'Help!' five or six times. No one answered: no one came – and his own voice seemed to linger unsuitably in the air. He looked to the coffin, now shrouded in darkness. Had he – had he waked the enormous dead?

Against the faint window he saw Black Jack's feet. They were rooted still in the same patch of air – standing, so to speak, half-way up the window pane ... He returned once more to his chair and rested his head against the fireplace wall.

Though he desired strongly to sleep out the hours remaining, sleep would not come. The presence in the coffin seemed to hold it at bay ... as if the great death shamed the little one and would not let it come.

Now, little by little, the moon climbed out of the invisible chimney pots, turning the window to dull silver, so that it hung in the dark wall like an old tarnished mirror, capable of nothing but spite.

With a sigh of relief Dorking heard a clock strike nine. His vigil was almost done. He stood up and began to walk softly about the room – to ease the cramp in his legs and ward off the night's chill.

The silver moonlight, very bright now, seemed to lend the dingy room an odd beauty – as if it was intricately fashioned out of shining grey lead. Even the coffin and the still ruffian within it seemed carved and moulded by a master hand.

How finely done was the tangled hair – the knotted brow – the powerful, thick nose ... how lifelike were the deep grey lips. How – how miraculously shone the moon in the profound eyes –

In the eyes? In the *eyes*? Sure to God those eyes had been shut before?

Those eyes! They were open wide! They were moving! They were staring at him!

Bartholomew Dorking, sent from Shoreham to London to be spared the perils of the sea, stood almost dead of terror.

'Alive!' he moaned. 'He's alive!'

More dreadful than violent death itself was this reviving from it.

A deep, rattling sigh filled the room. Black Jack's chest heaved – and his box crackled ominously. His moon-filled eyes rolled fiercely at Bartholomew.

'Alive!' groaned the boy. 'He's alive!' Where was the widow who might have been rejoiced by the awful sight? Back in half an hour. Black Jack's head twitched and shook and strove to rise. His mouth gaped wide and his eyes rolled downward – as if to point some queer dilemma he was in.

With such relief as he was capable of, the boy saw that the monstrous ruffian was helpless. His arms were wedged into the box. Till he burst the wood, he was securely coffined. Again his eyes, like a pair of silver prisoners frantically pressing their

17

confines, turned upon the boy, then back towards the gaping mouth. He coughed somewhat awkwardly – as if he would speak, but could not. Then he drew several deep breaths that came and went with a thin fluting whistle. His eyes – his terrible eyes – took on an anguished air . . .

Helplessly the boy drew near him. Despite his dread, the huge man's plight moved him.

'Y-you're alive, then?' he whispered.

For answer, Black Jack's mouth stretched wider yet – as if inviting the boy to climb inside and see for himself.

Black Jack's breath was not of the sweetest. His hearty breakfast was giving up its stinking ghost. But the boy continued to approach. It was plain the terrible man needed help – on account of something in the deep of his mouth.

Absorbed, the boy peered in. He fancied he could see a glint of metal in the yawning throat. Black Jack's eyes were now frantic in their appeal. The boy pointed to what he thought he'd seen. Black Jack strained to nod.

There was an obstruction of sorts. He desired Bartholomew Dorking, draper's apprentice, to put his hand into his huge mouth and ease out the cause of his distress. The boy groaned – but obliged.

With infinite caution – and dreading that, if he made an ill-judged move the ruffian would snap his hand off at the wrist – he drew out a bent silver tube some half an inch wide and four inches long.

This tube had been the cause of Black Jack's outliving Mr Ketch's rope. He'd wedged it in his throat as a preventative against strangulation. But his own huge weight had dented it grievously; and it had nearly done for him of its own accord.

The boy dropped the tube with a sob of relief; then he stepped back, thankful that they'd both survived the surgery. Black Jack glared at him; then he winked and grinned.

'Where – am – I, mister?' His voice was ragged and hoarse, and came with much wincing – as if speech was a torture devised by the devil.

The boy Dorking brightened. He had good news for the huge felon.

'Home, Mr Gorgandy. You're in your own parlour and home.'

'Home? Parlour? Gorgandy? This ain't my home. My name ain't Gorgandy. What are you at, mister?'

Thinking Black Jack to've been unsettled by his frightful experience, Bartholomew confided gently that his widow, or, rather, his wife would be back in half an hour. And with all his kith and kin. To drink his health. Wasn't that a handsome thing to come? Wasn't that a cause for happy smiling? Picture their amazed delight! Picture Mrs G's tearful happiness! Picture the genial night to come!

Bartholomew's good-natured heart warmed and his eyes sparkled as he imagined the prospects of Seven Blackfriars Lane.

'And there'll be Doctor Hunter and Doctor Skimpole, too –'

Black Jack's face, which had been entirely bewildered, abruptly took on a look of murderous rage.

'Gorgandy!' he muttered. 'Is she that fat black bag what hangs about the gallows' posts on nubbing Mondays? I know her now! I seed her there this very morning! So that's what it's about! So that's why I'm here! Rot her frowsy soul! Half an hour, did you say, mister? I must get out! Or she'll sell me, living, to damned Surgeons Hall!'

He began to struggle and heave till, with a mighty, splintering crash, the coffin split from side to side and Black Jack staggered free.

'Weak as a sucking baby!' he muttered, tenderly rubbing at his neck.

His hopes of a happy outcome dashed, Bartholomew Dorking crept to the door and prayed the enormous ruffian would overlook him.

'She'll not have me!' groaned Black Jack, now clutching his bruised arms. He tottered to the window, smashed it with his fist and seized hold of the iron bars.

'Weak – weak as a sucking baby!' he grunted and, with a calamitous clatter of masonry, wrenched the bars out of the anchoring bricks.

'Mister!' (With a chill, Bartholomew understood he'd not been overlooked.) 'Over here, mister!'

'W-why, Black Jack?'

'You're coming with me.'

'W-why, Black Jack?'

'I'll not have you bawling the odds that Black Jack ain't dead, mister. Let the old bag think you've sold me on your own account, eh?' He tried to laugh but found it too painful. 'Besides, I needs you, mister – till I gets back my health and strength. I'm weak, mister. Weak as a sucking baby.'

Thereupon, he seemed but to lean across the room, seize the boy by his arm and neck and hoist him briefly through the gaping window into the cold and deathly moonlight.

2

AT nine o'clock Mr Hardcastle, draper of Ludgate Hill, bolted his door and led his family up to bed.

'Them that roisters on the Town all night, sleeps in the freezing street,' he said, meaning his apprentice, Dorking, who'd elected to play the dirty stop-out and so botch the good opinion his shining manner had won.

At ten o'clock Mrs Gorgandy unlocked her parlour door and led in several grave gentlemen of cautious aspect and medicinal smell. Speechless, she surveyed her broken, tumbled room.

'Took in!' she shrieked. 'I been took in! Advantage! 'Ee took advantage, good sirs! And 'ee looked so shining kind and honest! Two shillings 'ee 'ad off me – and Mister Ketch's makes three! Sold me out, that's what 'ee's done. Sold me out to low-class body-snatchers through the winder! And 'ee looked such a simple little soul ... Oh, 'ow I 'ates a yippercrit! If only 'ee'd looked more villainous, gents, if only –'

The object of this shocked dismay – the causer, so to speak, of this loss of faith in human nature – crouched in a dingy yard, some six old walls west of Mrs Gorgandy's ruined window. Beside him loomed the granite bulk of Black Jack, whose menacing head – angled oddly on account of his damaged neck – stood poised against the sky like a rock about to come tumbling down and crush the boy to death.

Bartholomew shivered. Try as he might to keep in charity, he could not help longing, with all his heart, that his grim companion was back in his coffin in Mrs Gorgandy's parlour. Not that he wanted Black Jack dead so much as wishing most profoundly that he'd never come back to life.

It was possible that the huge man divined these thoughts, for he frowned down on the terrified boy with some savagery and contempt.

'Pie,' he grunted. 'Give me the pie, mister.'

Hastily, Bartholomew handed over Mrs Gorgandy's veal pie (which had been thrust into his arms through the window). Black Jack seized it and began to stuff it into his mouth, muttering the while about 'his health and strength'. He chewed vigorously, then attempted to swallow. At once he gave a cry of distress and spat the pie out in a shower. He cursed and swore with harsh desperation. The violence done to his throat and neck by Mr Ketch had been severe. He was not able to eat.

'Apothecary!' he groaned. 'You got to fetch me to an apothecary, mister. You ain't going on your way till I got back me health and strength. So there's no call for you to roll your eyes like bleeding marbles looking for a bolt-hole. There ain't one. Remember, mister, though I'm weak as

a sucking baby, I'm yet more'n enough to thump you into a pudding.'

An apothecary, thought Bartholomew dismally; where in God's name was he to find such a thing?

As far as he'd been able to see, when he'd been briefly up (under Black Jack's helpful arm), had stretched the curious landscape of the town within the town. The secret and midnight yards and gardens that marched and rose and fell and tumbled darkly among the backs of houses and frowning tenements. Here and there, frightful under the moon, had glimmered the wizened effigy of a tree – very starved and ill-looking, as if it was not so much rooted as manacled to the invisible ground, maybe to prevent it from running for its piti-ful life to some more spacious plot, away from the muddle of walls.

Walls there'd been of every size and condition; fat walls, thin walls, old, slouching walls that loitered – with no intent – between walls with broken glass teeth that grinned and glittered under the moon.

Somewhere, over one of these walls, there must have been – in the very nature of things – the yard or garden of an apothecary. But over which?

'On our way, mister,' grunted Black Jack rearing up. 'I pins me faith in you. I leans on you – in a manner of speaking.'

He laid his hand on Bartholomew's shoulder, rested it there for a moment, then gripped into the boy's very bone and hoisted him to his feet. He glanced up to the night sky.

'Pick on a star, mister. Follow it – and I hopes, for your sake no less than mine, it turns out to be one with an apothecary's blink.'

Bartholomew followed Black Jack's glance. Glumly he traced out the sky's faint perforations. Even as he did so, a star fell like a loose thread and was snipped off into nothing.

'God have mercy on all at sea,' he muttered from habit; for his uncle, the ship's captain, had ever told him that, whenever a star is snuffed, a vessel has gone down with all souls aboard her.

Black Jack, who heard the mutter but not the words, most likely took it for an oath. He scowled murderously, and Bartholomew, in a sudden access of fear and loneliness, wondered if his uncle was out, watching the stars; and if, when he saw one fall to extinction, he'd guess it marked the loss of a draper's apprentice, gone down in a stinking back yard.

'Which way, mister?'

Suddenly the boy spied out the North Star. By its light seafarers had always set their courses. Why not, then, a draper's apprentice? Southward he'd go. Sixty miles to the south was his uncle's house and the Sussex sea. Maybe he'd no great hopes of reaching them, but his longing to do so at that moment was powerful and profound. Of Mr Hardcastle in

Ludgate Hill, he'd not a thought. His draper's life had been cut off before it had properly begun.

'This way, Mister Jack,' whispered Bartholomew, turning his back to the North Star. 'I've got a – a feeling for this way, sir.'

So it was that they began their creeping, scrambling, urgent journey towards the south. Over the cruel walls they went, dropping down into the cells of darkness between, with the boy nosing desperately for a whiff of herbs or aromatic spirits that would betray the whereabouts of an apothecary. But the night reeked only of old fish, old meat, old cabbage and many another aged thing, long past an apothecary's caring.

'I got a pain, mister!' groaned Black Jack each time he heaved the boy aloft. 'A strangling, choking, squeezing pain!' And his huge hands would press into the boy's ribs as if to force them into his lungs and heart. 'What d'you see, mister? What d'you smell?'

'Stinking mutton, Mister Jack – and there's a house that's tipping like a – a beached wreck. But the next one looks more – more prosperous, sir.'

Indeed they were very like forgotten hulks, creaking at dry anchor in their dock gardens – these tall, dark, makeshift backs of houses – with, here and there, lines of light drawn round shutters like the remnants of gilding on high old poops ... A once mighty fleet left stranded by a sea that had fled, long, long ago, sixty miles to the south. Why, there even dipped lines of what might have been pennants (had it not been washing instead), which seemed to fly sad signals to the watchful moon.

From one of these lines hung a gown of glum worsted, supernaturally large on account of its dampness.

'Wait there, mister,' growled Black Jack, and cut the garment down. Mr Ketch had left him half naked to the chilly night, believing he'd have no further occasion to shiver in it.

He began to put the garment on but, large as it was, Black

25

Jack was still larger and there came a sound of spitting and splitting as he fought his way in.

Very queer was the sight that met Bartholomew's eyes: in the interrupted moonlight (some smallish clouds having gone across the moon), the gigantic fellow seemed to've been suddenly caught in a life-after-death struggle with a malignant ghost that hissed and flapped and sought to engulf him. Up went Black Jack's arms, and up went the ghost's. Then Black Jack's head was swallowed to the neck, and a turmoil went on in the ghost's belly – as if it had bitten off more than it could chew. Which suddenly proved to be the case. Black Jack's head and hands came out against the sky and the confusion died. The gown hung meek and torn from the huge man's shoulders, giving him a strangely monkish air.

'You was saying, mister – you'd got hopes of an apothecary – where?'

Following the brief wisps, a somewhat slower, grosser cloud passed across the moon, like a grandfather limping after children ... The boy and the giant felon stared towards each other. In the one pair of eyes was savagery, contempt, even murder – and an angry bitterness that he should be obliged to the white-faced maggot of an apprentice who peered up at him. In the boy's eyes there was fear of savagery, fear of murder and also a glint of bitterness provoked by the felon's contempt. Then the cloud was gone and the boy climbed up unaided on to a wall and stared along the backs of the houses.

'Three – no, four walls off, Mister Jack.'

'What, mister?'

'There's a line with two aprons on it.'

'Aprons, mister? I got no need of them.'

'Apothecaries wear aprons, Mister Jack.'

'So do carpenters, mister.'

'But they don't wash 'em, Mister Jack.'

'Hm – get moving, mister. And pray.'

26

The yard where the aprons hung stank no better or worse than its neighbours. Two cats with angry eyes left their business and fled as the night travellers dropped down.

A quantity of yellow light was coming from between the ill-fitting shutters of a brick extension that had been applied to the back of the house like a poultice. (Indeed, many of the houses hereabouts had brick or wood outgrowths to them – as if the rooms had gone varicose with too long standing.)

The boy crept to the window and peered through the shutters. He saw a stout, elderly man, filthy in aspect and bald as an apple, at a deal table upon which were a number of stoneware pots, a quill and inkwell – and a pestle and mortar.

'An apothecary!' breathed Bartholomew, as if it was the most marvellous of God's creations.

'Then bid him tend me!' snarled Black Jack. 'Else you and him's for the worms!'

There was a narrow, arched passageway between the apothecary's house and its neighbour. Through it now passed the boy and the crouching giant.

With enormous caution they came out into the street where the genteel houses, standing shoulder to shoulder, seemed to be blandly denying that filth, confusion and shambling ruin could possibly dwell behind their pinned-on frontages.

The apothecary's windows were shuttered, but above hung a gilded pestle and mortar – which sign of his trade was also on his front door, fashioned in brass for a knocker, so that the pestle banged upon the mortar.

Bartholomew raised his hand to knock. Even as he did so, Black Jack's shadow engulfed him and fell across the door, so that the loud, hollow sound seemed to be caused, not by the knocker, but by the great shadow striking upon the door – for all the world as if it possessed weight, substance – and menace.

The apothecary was a long time coming; but his voice was heard almost directly, from the deep of his house.

'Coming ... coming! Directly, now! Don't go off! I'll be

with you ... coming myself ... servants abed, d'you see! No matter ... always at the disposal of the sick! Coming ... just a moment, now –'

Came a sound of a bolt sliding back, a chain unfastened – a key turned. The door opened and the apothecary, quite transformed by a black coat and a Dutch wig, stared at the disturber of his peace. Almost at once, as if he'd come out wearing the wrong face, he changed that, too – from kindly concern to angry disappointment.

He did not see Black Jack, who kept in the entrance to the passageway, but only the boy – torn, muddy, uneasy looking. Was this the customer? Then damn him for an impudent lout!

'He needs – needs your help,' muttered Bartholomew; and the apothecary's face suffered a further change as Black Jack moved out and towered against the sky. So abrupt and extraordinary was his appearance, that he might have risen out of the ground.

'He can't eat – he can't swallow – he can't get his nourishment,' went on Bartholomew urgently.

The apothecary's alarm subsided. He'd seen that the huge, silent man wore a monkish kind of gown. He decided he was a mendicant friar, a charity-hawker, a Christian beggar of the worst and filthiest sort.

Also, he'd a shrewd notion that all he'd get in the way of payment from this enormous Brother, would be a feeble smile and a trumpery blessing ...

So (like his betters, the physicians) he began to be overbearing. He bade his callers be off; to come again at half after nine in the morning like the respectable halt and lame; that he was not at the beck and call of every dusty piece of worthlessness that the wind blew in; that –

Of a sudden he was amazed that the boy had laid a hand on him – was pushing him back through his own doorway – was pleading almost savagely with him!

'For God's sake, sir – tend this – this man! *Please!* I beg you – please tend him now!'

In a fury he was about to strike the boy, when, in the candle-light, he caught a glimpse of an extraordinary anguish in his eyes. In spite of his indignation he was much shaken. He conceived that the boy thought his companion was dying – and would stop at nothing to save him.

He had not seen the huge monk's fists clench, nor his shoulders heave. He did not know that Bartholomew Dorking was consumed with terror that Black Jack was about to murder the apothecary.

Grudgingly and somewhat sullenly, the apothecary said:

'For a minute, then. Only a minute, mark you. I'll take a look. Bring him into the shop. Bid him be careful – the monstrous great lout! Can't eat, you say? Can't swallow? Can't take his nourishment? Hm – hm – there's a lot of it about! Yes, indeed. Not uncommon, that.'

The shop was in the front parlour: a small, varnished room that seemed to be built out of varnished cupboards, varnished drawers with china handles and varnished shelves upon which were crowded – in supernatural numbers – pots, bottles, jars, beakers and flasks all reflecting the apothecary's candle with an air of obedient but nervous gloom.

'Bid him squat down. I ain't climbing up to see him. Squat him down in the corner.'

The apothecary pointed as Black Jack shambled into the room. Bartholomew gazed imploringly at the huge man, whose face was as stone. None the less he squatted.

'Bid him open his mouth. Wide.'

Like his betters, the physicians, the apothecary had the trick off pat of never addressing a patient save through a third party – as if sickness made them too ignorant to be spoken with direct.

Again, Bartholomew gazed at Black Jack – who opened his mouth with a deep groan. The apothecary drew close and held

29

his candle so that Black Jack's breath was seen streaming up – as if there was something boiling, deep in his vitals.

'Yes ... yes ...' muttered the apothecary, peering into the ragged throat. 'Abrasions – swellings – roughness ... as I suspected. It's going around, y'know. There's a deal of it about. But I've an oil that's soothing. Even so, you must warn him that it'll get worse before it gets better. But the oil will help. Ah! What's this? What's this I see?'

He'd stepped back and the candlelight had fallen on Black Jack's neck where, livid and fearful, was Mr Ketch's signature, that mark, so to speak, that denoted that Black Jack was being returned to his Maker with a complaint.

He bent forward to examine it, all but singeing Black Jack's beard with his candle. He laid his hand on the huge man's shoulder, unaware of the terror that had come into the boy's face as he did so.

Abruptly the apothecary stepped back. He wore a satisfied smile.

'A damp gown. That's what's done it. Abrased the skin. Painful; but not uncommon. Rheumatic neck. Seen it before; dozens of times. I've an ointment for it. Rub it in twice a day, and be cautious of wet clothing. Cost you – um – three shillings for the oil, the ointment and me time. Bid him shut his mouth and stand up now.'

The apothecary had turned to his shelves for the oil and the ointment and spoke somewhat carelessly over his shoulder. He did not concern himself to look round – which was as well, else he might not have spoken at all. He might, instead, have screamed aloud in a sudden and appalling fear of death.

Rearing up behind him, Black Jack stood, his great fists lifted to smash down upon his head.

'No – no! Please don't!' moaned Bartholomew.

Black Jack stared at the boy. His face, which was cruel and savage, took on a look of sneering contempt. He shrugged his shoulders and opened his fists.

'Don't what?' asked the apothecary turning about. He saw

the huge, monkish beggar whose hands were still upraised. 'He can bless me till kingdom come,' said the apothecary quite mistaking the giant's intent. 'Just so long as I get my money too.'

Outside in the street, some two or three minutes after parting with the apothecary and three shillings, there came to Bartholomew a piece of extraordinary good fortune ... a chance in a million, so to speak.

Moving as they did, away from the exposed middle of the street and close in the shadow of the houses, the murderous felon's gown had caught upon the spikes of some basement railings. He cursed and halted and began to disentangle himself.

Though the time was brief it was sufficient for the boy to bolt for his life. Indeed, every muscle and nerve in his body jumped to do so.

Yet he hesitated. It was certain that Black Jack saw the impulse – and observed it crushed. The sneering contempt that never left his face grew as deep and enormous as the night. The boy shuddered under the stinging weight of it. His feet scraped the cobbles; his hands sweated; every sense he possessed urged him, warned him to begone.

But a formidable chain had been forged between him and Black Jack. He dreaded what the murderous ruffian he'd resurrected would do in the world. It had been Bartholomew's pleading alone that had spared the apothecary. How many others was he doomed to save?

This was one link. Terror was another: terror of being followed, found out and savagely destroyed.

But the third link was different – seemingly slighter, yet perhaps the strongest of all. The very hugeness, strength and wildness of the giant awed the boy like a phenomenon in Nature. And in due proportion, his contempt was crushing and unendurable. More than anything else in the world, Bartholomew longed to change that contempt into respect. With all his heart and soul he craved for Black Jack's admiration.

At last Black Jack had freed himself. He sneered: 'You was going to make off, mister. But you'd never have got farther than a yard –'

'W-what d'you want with me now, Mister Jack?'

'Want with you?' The ruffian grinned – then put on an air of mocking servility. 'Oh, mister – I needs you by me ... to save me from sin, y'know. To save me from my murderous nature. It ain't every hanged felon what can travel with a whey-faced weasel of a saint. So you stays, mister. You stays till I says "go"!'

The boy scowled and shrugged his shoulders.

'And when will that be, Mister Jack?'

To which Black Jack answered with a stare of hatred. No more could the boy confess his need of the monster's admiration, than could Black Jack himself declare his need of the boy. He could not abide to continue under the obligation of his life – his strong, lawless and perversely proud life itself – to a creature so contemptible. He could not help himself. He must discharge the debt.

Thus they were opposed to the very depths of their souls. There was no possibility of resolution. The profoundest need of the one cancelled out the same in the other. Neither could climb out of his unrest save on the heart of his companion.

'What's your name, mister?' grunted Black Jack abruptly.

Bartholomew paused miserably. He'd have given much to've been called 'Brown Sam', or 'Green Joe', or even plain Joe or Tom, or Dick; anything, in short, that might have matched the rough strength of 'Black Jack'.

'Bartholomew Dorking,' he said at length in a low voice; and it seemed more than ever ridiculously fiddling and curly.

'Too long for so short a brat. So what'll I call you? Bart? No. Needs a man of some size – which you ain't got, mister. Barty, then? No. Needs a touch of nerve – which you ain't got either, mister. Tolly. That's it, mister. I'll call you Tolly. So it's which way, Tolly? Guide me, Tolly. Lead me in the way of salvation, Tolly.'

Bitterly the boy glanced up to the sky: but the stars were now obscured under a mottling of cloud.

'This way, then, Mister Jack,' he said, facing once more what he hoped was south. 'I've still got some hopes of this way...'

3

THEY moved with circumspection through the night; chose the infirm alleys and crippled lanes that slunk by the river in a blind and stinking confusion – as if the very streets were lost and would have cast themselves into the river if only they could have found the way.

They hastened over London Bridge and heard, far below, the loose water slap and cuddle the old piles in affectionate farewell on its way to the distant sea.

Now Southwark saw them – or would have done had it been awake; but the hour was close on two, and even the busy George Inn was wrapped in a decent sleep. Harness jingled faintly as they passed, and a horse snorted dreamily on the memory of some sudden plunge or a fine fall of road . . .

The boy walked a pace ahead of his enormous companion who seemed to hang over him like a menacing shadow. No talk passed between them – not even a casual word – and the only sounds they made were the shuffle and slap of their feet and the monster's breathing, which drowned out the quick, almost panting breath of the boy.

From time to time the man would give a sharp groan as the uneven cobbles caused him to jolt and jar his dreadful neck. Then the boy would turn, stare at him with involuntary concern, which changed directly to fear and resentment as he met the giant's implacable sneer and dark dislike.

At last the hedging houses were gone and they were come upon the Common at Clapham; a very wild and forlorn place . . . Here, by a clump of hawthorns, Black Jack anointed himself with the apothecary's ointment and sipped the soothing oil.

The bushes were dense and furnished some shelter from the night. The travellers glanced briefly at each other and settled down for the fag-end of the dark. The boy, quite worn out by the strains and alarms of his day, seemed to fall asleep directly. The giant was, perhaps, ten minutes in arrears.

At half after three, having heard the giant's regular breathing for some time, the boy cautiously opened his eyes.

'I ain't sleeping, Tolly. I was took when asleep, and I swore that never again would man or child come on me so.'

When it was light they set off again, much chilled from the clinging dew and plagued with hunger and thirst. A small inn, half a mile out of Clapham provided them with cheese and ale in exchange for Bartholomew's last sixpence. A quiet, respectable inn, with a quiet, respectable landlord and a little potboy to match. Inquisitively they watched as their huge, monkish customer lifted his tankard, drank – and swallowed.

On which they glared at one another in a sudden terror. What had they done? What had they served that morning? The little parlour fairly shook as the giant roared in agony!

Black Jack had broke his fast. The first victuals he'd taken since the breakfast of the condemned had gone safely, if painfully down. His health and strength were coming back.

'So God help me now,' thought the boy fearfully, after they'd left the inn and were walking beside the road. 'That's if God Himself is a match for such a man!'

Black Jack's health and strength seemed to have but a single aim: robbery and murder whenever a living soul crossed his shaking path.

'You're milk, Tolly – skimmed milk!' he sneered at the boy's pleading for the life of a farmer who rode, unsuspecting by.

'How many more?' wondered Bartholomew miserably. 'How many more will he spare before him and me's done?'

About a mile to the north of Croydon the road began to twist and turn as if it had got into a panic over where it was going. At first it was tolerably wide, but, by the third bend it had grown narrow and plunged between a high grass bank and a wood of beeches and birch closely set. This third bend was treacherous – even infamous : a place of common disaster.

Of which there was a sample awaiting the boy and the lumbering felon as they came abruptly into view.

A coach was tipped over into the ditch and its occupants, much dishevelled, were struggling to heave it upright. Some way off the coachman – somewhat damaged about the face and head from his meeting with the ground – was tending his horses who fidgeted and kept turning round to peer at the foundered coach which they were unable to assist, the road's surface being too loose for their hooves to get a purchase and pull the equipage out.

Black Jack seized Bartholomew's arm.

'I knew you was saving me up for something, Tolly.' He grinned savagely. 'For ain't this a rich gift come of your praying? Oh, me little saint! What luck you've brought me!'

'W-what are you going to do, Black Jack?'

The ruffian had picked up a broken branch of murderous weight.

'There's but five of 'em, Tolly. Shot-gun's on the roof. I don't see no pistols anywheres. So I'm a-going in, Tolly. I'm a-going in with me little stick. Cover your eyes, Tolly, if you puke at blood – for you can't crack heads without spilling it.' He paused reflectively, as if savouring a memory, then added : 'Or maybe you'll come with me, eh?'

His great wicked face was suddenly close to the boy, blotting out the world and all but killing him with foul breath. '*Will* you come?'

His chance was now. He'd but to join with Black Jack in bloody murder – not even to kill, perhaps, but to stand red-handed by – for those deep, contemptuous eyes to widen in respect and surprise. But unluckily his uncle, the sea-captain, had been right when he'd spoken of his too-soft heart. It wasn't the blood that made him puke, but the grief and misery that flowed in its wake.

'Let me go!' he muttered. 'Let me go – let me go –'

He tore himself free and fled towards the crippled coach. He heard the monster curse him and begin to pursue. He'd no thoughts of betraying Black Jack. Such thoughts as he'd time for in the whirling moment were grimmer and more desperate.

The strugglers at the coach looked up. Pleasure broke on their sweaty faces. Help was running at them – an eager boy and, in his wake, a most gigantic monk or friar or something else oddly dressed and charitably inclined. They waved, shouted: 'All hands welcome! You, lad – to the back and heave!'

To the back fled Bartholomew, where the coach tipped crazily and its roof came down to the ground.

'Heave!' cried the toilers – and wondered ruefully why the extra pair of hands made no odds.

Pressed against the coach's dipping wall, eyes fixed on the immovable ground, they could not see how the extra pair of hands was occupied.

Tolly had got at the shot-gun. From fifteen yards Black Jack saw him. He stopped; scowled uneasily, licked his lips . . .

'Come on, man!' shouted the sweating gentry, ignorant of the circumstance of the huge fellow's hesitating.

He grinned furtively. His eyes were screwed up as if the sun was in them. But there was no sun. Would the boy shoot him? No deep student of human nature, Black Jack took the glummest view of it. A look of eerie meekness came over his face. He shook his head. (You wouldn't harm poor Black Jack? Not Black Jack what you saved from a death worse'n fate?) He dropped his weapon and came sidling on.

The aching gentlemen gave over heaving. They beamed at the giant in wonderment and hope.

Behind them, half hid by the fallen wheel, the boy kept up the shot-gun. He was in two minds – and both of them desperate.

'Morning, gentlemen,' said Black Jack affably. 'Though I'm not in full health and strength – on account of a – a misfortune

– I'll do what I can for you. Move aside, there. Give me room to heave...'

He cast a brief glance towards the boy. An odd glance ... partly proud, partly cunning ...

'And for mercy's sake, Master Tolly, put down that bleeding cannon afore it goes off and does some innocent soul a mischief.'

Everyone looked round, wonderfully surprised.

'It – it fell off the roof,' mumbled the boy; and, biting his lip in shame and anger, put the shot-gun down.

Now the gigantic fellow laid his back against the side of the coach and, with the others, began to strain.

'Not – in – me – full – health an' strength!'

With a creaking and rumbling and scraping the coach began to shift.

'I'm – weak ... weak – as – as a babe, gents!'

On which the gentry collapsed as the coach shuddered sharply back on to the road.

'Bless 'is 'orny 'ands and mighty back!' panted the coachman, delicately wiping the blood from his chin with his sleeve. 'Come, gents – a whip-round ... a c'lection ... a donation for the Brother 'ere, and 'is little mate. Dip into yer pockets – for, if it weren't for our two good friends, we might all 'ave been set on and murdered to death while we were stuck 'ere!'

'Three pounds seventeen shillings and a pair of silver buckles,' said Bartholomew delightedly, after the coach was gone on its way and he and Black Jack were sat by the roadside, counting out the charity. 'And all got without harming a living soul. Ain't it easier this way, Mister Jack?'

There was more than a touch of satisfaction in Bartholomew's voice – and a look of the same on his face. His uncle, the sea-captain, had brought him up to be law-abiding, God-fearing and respectable; which schooling, acting upon his fatal softness of heart, gave him – at such times as this – a feeling of heart-deep virtue capable of provoking offence.

But not, it seemed, to Black Jack. The ruffian nodded as best he was able, picked some pebbles from between his toes, and squinted thoughtfully at the boy.

'Oh yes, Tolly – you was right. As I always said – lucky is that hanged felon what has a saint to bear him company. You have shown me the way, Tolly dear. You have improved me. Not Black Jack any more, but Grey Jack, eh?'

He stood up and began to shift a large, jagged stone with his foot. Then he bent down and picked it up.

'What are you at, Mister Jack?'

'You've shown me the way, Tolly,' he said with a vicious grin; then went to lay the stone in the road at the deadliest part of that deadly bend. No coach passing could fail to strike on it and be overturned.

'And now for the next load of grateful gents!'

'Damn you!' whispered Bartholomew, dismally picturing the broken backs and necks and screams and shrieks and piteous sights to come; and then seeing the implacable ruffian leering at him in high contempt. 'You foul, stinking murderer! I wish they'd hanged you properly! Oh God, I wish –'

It seemed that a thunderclap struck him on the side of his head. He flew over and fell into the ditch.

Black Jack had hit him with his open hand and all but broken his temples open.

With his head burning and his eyes streaming with tears he crawled back. The terrible, huge man was staring at him.

'You stop your squealing and whining to God, Tolly. He won't do you no good when I'm about. You just count yourself lucky me fist wasn't clenched and your brains ain't over the grass. You hold your tongue, Tolly, and do as you're bid; or I'll break you in two.'

Bitterness and fury filled the boy to choking – for he dared not show them. Instead, he crouched down beside the enormous mockery of a monk.

'What was that you said, Tolly?'

'Nothing.'

'I got sharp ears, Tolly. I hears a whisper. I sometimes hears a thought, maybe. I fancied I heard you swear you'd get even with me, Tolly. Was it so?'

The boy held his peace, and tried to keep his eyes to himself. Black Jack went on and, in his dark, violent face, there was a look of unfathomable hate.

'Then just remember this, Tolly. Remember it well. Not as long as you live will you get even with me. So don't never try. Just bide with me till I'm done with you – then go snivelling where you like. Now, Tolly, down in this long grass . . . till the next coach comes. And then –'

So they crouched – and waited.

*

In a spacious mansion about a mile outside of Reigate, lived the Carter family – in easy circumstances but cursed by God. There was madness within their doors.

They kept few servants, did the Carters, and paid them well for their loyalty and discretion. But of a consequence, many of the upstairs rooms were abandoned to dust and shutters, giving the mansion's handsome frontage an oddly purblind air . . .

Behind one of these shuttered windows dwelt the demented creature – the 'poor thing' – whose presence hung over the mansion like a menacing shadow.

'Poor thing' had first been the servants' description, but now it was used by all, as if to diminish the horror into a trifling piece of ill-luck. (But there was a footman whose face and arms had borne marks of injury for weeks after infliction who said 'poor thing' with a very ironical pity indeed.)

None the less, this easy-circumstanced family managed to live in their world with a pride that did much to cover up the calamity with which they'd been cursed. It would have needed a wonderfully shrewd observer to see the shadows that lurked at the backs of their eyes – as if, somewhere in the deep of their minds, a black moth was for ever fluttering its wings . . .

They seemed to live so much in the broad day – to be so much

out and about in Reigate society and beyond – that it was hard to believe they had anything to hide.

Yet at quiet four o'clock in the morning of April fifteen, six candles were flickering in the principal parlour, casting their light on a curious scene.

The master and mistress of the house – looking as pale as caught thieves – were standing as if to wrap themselves in the room's thick shadows. They had three visitors; secret, serious and dusty gentlemen, all in black.

The 'poor thing' from upstairs – the Carter's curse – was to be removed from the house at last and be taken into the care of Dr Jones – who had a private Bedlam in Islington – at the rate of fifty guineas a year.

Together with Dr Jones was come his coachman, Mitchell, and his chaplain, adviser and friend, Parson Hall. This Parson Hall was a lean, blue-jowled, prophetical-looking gentleman whose pale eyes and stern demeanour the Carters found to be the most disquieting things in the room. Not that he said much, beyond murmurings of 'God's punishment' and 'Divine Retribution' ... as if to impress the comfortable Carters that they were getting quite a bargain in ridding themselves of so awesome a thing for only fifty guineas a year.

On the other hand, Dr Jones, a shorter, stouter, cleaner man altogether, spoke out much more about the merits of his establishment. Seclusion ... quiet ... good food ... handsome ground ... attention ... absolute discretion ... the 'poor thing' would be happy ... no need to worry ... etc., etc.

'If we don't get moving, gentlemen, it'll be daylight before we're away.'

Mitchell, the coachman, interrupted his master, and got a nod of approval from Parson Hall.

Mrs Carter sighed and whispered to a footman (the same who'd once been injured) who went directly to help bring the 'poor thing' down and out of the house.

The creature had to be removed secretly, as if such a curse had never been. The reason for this was, most ironically, that a blessing was in the offing. The Carters' daughter, Kate, had caught his eye and interest of a certain Lord Somers (on the other side of Reigate). Already Lord Somer's father had spoken with Mr Carter ... had made inquiries about Mr Carter's circumstances. And now Lord Somers himself – head over ears in love – was only waiting the outcome of the inquiries (which Mr Carter was assured was favourable) to ask Miss Carter's hand in marriage.

This was the blessing: but the Carters knew that it would never be theirs as long as a certain upstairs room was haunted by their 'poor thing'. For who would marry where madness was?

At a quarter after four it was done. God knows how the 'poor thing' was deceived into helping the general secrecy by not howling! All that remained in the hallway was a small hamper secured by straps that contained the 'poor thing's' worldly possessions. Then this, too, was lifted up by the footman – who never quite stopped looking ironical – and taken out of the house for ever. The curse was lifted; the Carters were available to be blessed.

Outside in the dark drive, Mitchell the coachman twitched the reins and the neat black coach grunted and crackled away over the gravel, drawn by two horses who nodded from side to side as if to an invisible crowd.

Very soon the equipage was out on the road and going at a spanking pace; Mitchell, high on his box, had something of Parson Hall's fire in his eyes ... as if he was imagining himself to be some legendary, even ghostly, coachman, whirling away the sins and misfortunes and curses of a frightened world.

By nine o'clock the black coach had rattled through Croydon, with Mitchell deeper than ever in his legendary dream. The road twisted and turned like a creature in torment and Mitchell's cheeks glowed and his eyes burned as he dreamed of flying across storm and whirlwind and earthquake and a general muddle of Divine Retribution with his shiny black casket of madness.

The coach rocked frantically as he took each turn – which suited his mood remarkably well. Then, quite suddenly, there was a fearful jolt. The whole equipage seemed to leave the road, remain hanging in the air for a brief moment, till it tilted and fell, with a wild noise, into the ditch!

It had struck on a large, jagged stone and gone, roof over wheels off its course. The horses screamed and dragged at their traces as if to escape the calamity. A storm of dust came up under their scrabbling hooves. Which hid a second disaster.

A door had burst open and the coach's contents were tumbled violently out. Mitchell, the coachman, lay in the road, dazed from a clout on the head and fancying he'd been capsized by one of his own imaginary whirlwinds, and that all the curses of Providence were loosed out of his black casket.

'The lunatic's gone!' came a scream from the ditch. 'Hall! Quick, man! Among the trees, I think! I can't move! It's in your hands now! Quick – before it's too late! My leg – it's broke...'

But Parson Hall was no better off than Dr Jones. Some violence had been done to his shoulder. Also there was blood on his face, beading out of long lacerations – as if he'd been surprised by something wild: a hawk, or a cat – or even the clawed hand of a briar...

Then, into this unlucky confusion, came help perhaps more sinister than the disaster itself. It was help that made the dazed Mitchell dream that the end of the world was closer at hand than he'd supposed.

Out of the storming dust had appeared a huge, monkish figure with black-bearded head on the tilt – as if it had been newly hanged – and a white-faced boy at its side, like a familiar spirit.

'Want any help, gents, in getting back on the road?' asked Black Jack with a murderously charitable grin.

4

TOLLY would have stayed to help the injured. His uncle, the sea-captain – before he'd hit on drapery for the boy's trade and shut his ears to the sea's calling – had often shown him how to bind up broken limbs. But the evil ruffian who'd brought on the disaster had dispatched him into the wood to search for the lunatic.

'You ain't frightened of a poor, mad thing, Tolly?' he'd sneered softly. 'Not Tolly what raised a man from the dead?'

There was good reason for Black Jack's concern. Dr Jones, clutching his knee, had groaned of a ten-pound reward. For a moment the helpless travellers might have perished for that ten pound – and whatever else they happened to have about them. Black Jack's eyes had glittered sharply when the sum was mentioned. Till Parson Hall – maybe on account of being in the trade, so to speak, and so not deceived by the monster's monkish gown – had spoken up quickly. Swore they'd but two pound fifteen between them. But pledged his very soul the rest would be their gentle rescuers' when they got home. If they got home. His pale, prophetical eyes burned with urgent hope . . .

Whereupon Black Jack had chewed on his lip and looked enormously cunning. At last he nodded and dispatched his familiar spirit to seek the mad creature among the shifting trees.

The wood which, at the outset, had been close, dark and sullen, seemed suddenly invaded with a fall of burning golden arrows. The April sun had broken out and was spiking through the upper leaves. Directly, a continuous and confused rustling began – from mysterious black holes in the bracken, from mouths in the wrinkled trunks of trees long dead, and from the creeping air behind him.

Tolly paused; had some thoughts of returning to the roadside and swearing the lunatic was gone. Then, on considering how he'd be received, abandoned them.

Cautiously he moved still deeper into the wood, feeling, of a sudden, much alone and unlucky in the world. Everything was larger, more violent and eerily grander than he. His virtues – such as they were – seemed of no more consequence than a paper boat on the roaring tide. Of what help was it to be God-fearing when he feared Black Jack so much the more? Of what help was his respectability against a raging lunatic? And by what laws was he now to abide?

Again he stopped, fancied a pair of glaring eyes watching him through the leaves.

He'd seen a lunatic once: a brandy merchant dragged raging from his ruined shop. A disquieting sight – even in a busy Shoreham street. In a lonely wood it would be more arresting. Even stupendous.

But the glaring eyes twittered and vanished, being no more than young leaves caught momentarily in the bright sun. A lunatic's eyes, the boy recalled, would have burned and rolled more. A lunatic would already have leaped on him and begun to strangle him with thin white fingers. A lunatic would –

He grew very cold. His heart faltered. His breath came awkwardly. He would have fled – but sensed that his legs would not bear his weight for much longer. A hand had touched him on the shoulder.

He commended his spirit to God – and hoped his prayer would get there before his soul. He turned. He stared directly into the face of the lunatic – the 'poor thing' – the Carters' curse! It was the face of a girl, scarcely fourteen.

Like a stone, the boy's terror sank into a sea of pity (yet contrived to leave behind some ripples of uneasiness). This girl, skinny, wispy, dusty as she was – with countenance as bland as white paper – was yet demented, vacant and uncanny.

She wore a green woollen cloak with a bulky hood in which her face nested like a butterfly in an old cabbage; and she stood in a patch of sunlight that made her look dustier than ever. She coughed slightly, as if the dust from her person had got into her throat. Then she smiled brightly and said: 'Would I really be better off dead?'

'Give me your hand,' muttered the boy, his heart suddenly wrung by the sombre question which the girl must many times have overheard. 'I'll take you back to – to the coach.'

She made to take his hand, when Tolly drew back for an instant. Her fingers were speckled with red. He shivered as he remembered that one of the traveller's faces had been a trifle torn. But the girl only looked puzzled. Then she smiled again – very radiantly. Indeed, she had a singularly beautiful smile that was quite bewitching.

'It's all right, you know. I been good and clean. I used the privy and washed proper. Swear to God and hope to die.'

Gently, Bartholomew took her hand and began to lead her back towards the road.

As they walked she laughed and chattered a good deal – as if they were the oldest of friends and their meeting not in the least remarkable. Indeed, nothing seemed remarkable to her, for her memory was too brief to make a wonder. Though all seemed new, nothing seemed strange. Had the trees flown up, trailing their roots, had the ground cracked wide and horned devils crept screaming out, Bartholomew felt that her face would still have stayed bland as white paper ... waiting for something more striking to be written on it.

Yet here and there, in her quick, loud chatter, came shafts of something else. Her voice would change and she'd speak evenly and plainly, as if she'd come upon some islands of memory in her unrippled mind ... or as if her brain itself was veiled in dust which, in spots, had been rubbed away.

'I would be better off dead, you know...' Or, 'I'm a poor thing what steals and spits and has horrible dirty habits. You want to watch out for me, you do...' Or again, 'I'm a curse to

47

the master and mistress and it's a shame. I must be God's punishment, I must. Wouldn't it be a blessing if I was to do myself a mischief and come to a merciful end?'

Yet even these fearful memories of whisperings overheard were attended by no more than a look of childish cunning and pride at having eavesdropped and not been caught. It was plain she'd no notion of their import.

They walked very slowly – for the girl was wayward and apt to pull and heave Tolly off his course. Three or four times they went in a circle and came back to the same patch of sunlight in which stood a holly, grown quaintly like a tent. This tree fascinated the mad girl. Suddenly she broke free and ran, flickering in the chequered sun, to crouch down within this tent. She looked up, and sideways, then stared fixedly ahead. For the first time her face looked troubled. She frowned and bit her lip as if trying to catch at something that hovered on the tip of her mind.

'What's wrong?' asked the boy, kneeling beside her.

'D'you see it?' she whispered.

'What – where?'

'A tall black tower with a golden top – higher than the sky. There are white angels flying with white wings. And all the world's singing a lullaby – for the sun's gone to bed in a blanket. D'you see it now?'

'No,' said Tolly honestly: and was entirely unprepared for what followed. With the speed and fierceness of a cat, the mad girl flew at him with feet, fists and nails!

She sobbed and screamed and panted in the violence of her fury – till the amazed boy had recovered himself enough to escape the worst. Then, more angry than frightened – for his face and the backs of his hands were bleeding pretty freely – he seized hold of her wrists.

She fought, and, being mad, fought with the strength of ten. But mercifully none of the ten was very strong, so Tolly prevailed.

'You're mad – mad!' he panted at last – and the girl, quite

imprisoned in her heavy cloak whose hood had slipped back to free a quantity of dusty, reddish hair, smiled blandly up at him.

'They call me Belle,' she said brightly. 'What do they call you?'

'Tolly,' said Bartholomew, so thrown out by the rapid change of mood that he forgot to say 'Bartholomew Dorking'. But then, he reflected, it didn't really matter. She wouldn't be with him much longer, so it signified little what she called him. He helped her to her feet.

'Come, Belle. I remember now which way the road is. Soon you'll be back with – with your friends.'

So, hand in hand, they left the green and golden wood and presently came back to the side of the road.

True to her incomplete nature, she did not look surprised. Indeed, what in the world was there to surprise one who had neither memory nor expectation? Why should she look any way but peaceable at so ordinary a thing as a road?

But Tolly, on the other hand, had reasons. He looked startled half out of his wits. The road was empty! The coach was gone: the travellers were gone – and so was the murdering giant.

Nothing remained but a muddle of wheel tracks to show where the coach had gone off the road – and then been heaved back on to it. All there was left of the calamity was a small hamper, secured with straps, half hid in the ditch.

'Mister Jack?' called the boy nervously. 'Black Jack?'

Nothing answered, nothing stirred – save the long grass on the opposing slope as the wind moved quietly through it. The huge man must have gone off with the travellers – most likely to batter them to death in the more profitable seclusions of their own home. Foolish gentlemen! They need never have spoke of their ten pound. Black Jack would have obliged by killing them for much less.

Tolly shouted again, not knowing whether he really wanted the monster to appear and plague him once more with humiliation and dread. But there was no Black Jack, and Belle, unconcerned, had opened the hamper and was laying out her pitiful possessions – tattered dolls, cheap trinkets and wretched linen – along the road's edge, with little coughs and cries of pleasure and pride.

'Where do you come from, Belle?' asked Tolly at length, with a desperation he tried hard to conceal.

She looked up at him with her aggravatingly pretty smile. 'From where you found me, Tolly.'

Patiently he sighed, and tried again.

'Where do you live, Belle?'

'Here,' she said, pointing to her breast. 'This is where we all live, don't you know? If you listen, you can hear there's someone at home ... knocking.'

She shrugged her shoulders and returned to smoothing out a child's gown that had been let out and unfashionably added to.

'What's your name, then?' persisted Tolly, striving not to grow irritable with the lunatic.

'Belle. I told you. And you're Tolly. Ain't that so?'

'Have you no other name, Belle?'

She thought deeply. 'Yes.'

'What is it?' (Here was a glimmer of hope at last!)

'Sometimes they call me "Poor thing",' said the girl with a proud smile.

'Oh my God,' muttered Tolly and, shovelling the mad girl's rubbish back into the hamper, fastened it and hoisted it on his back.

'We might as well go south again, Belle,' he sighed. 'My uncle, the sea-captain, will know what to do.'

As they moved off, hand in hand along the road's edge, Bartholomew fancied he glimpsed – out of the corner of his eye – something dark and huge stir in the long grass.

'Black Jack?' he called softly. But the grass was still again – save for the attentions of the breeze – and no one answered.

So they went on and did not look back. Belle was smiling, but Tolly looked vaguely troubled, for he could not rid himself of a feeling of being watched – and followed.

5

THOUGH much to be preferred to the evil Black Jack, Belle was not the most superior of walking companions. Her gait, though not at all awkward, was unusual. Her step being very springing, she tended to rise and fall somewhat playfully by Tolly's side, with her ancient green cloak flapping like the wings of some enormous, mildewed moth.

Being of a very genteel upbringing, Tolly felt the embarrassment shrewdly; and it was made the more painful by the grins of oafish farm labourers – of whom there seemed to be an unnatural number about that morning. So, just before Croydon, they turned off the highway into a quiet and obscure lane that led to Ewell, which was still – though roundabout – on the way to the Sussex sea.

Just before they did so, Tolly looked briefly back – as if still troubled by the sense of being followed. But there was no huge shape to be seen ... and the long grass was quiet ... even unusually so.

Was it possible, he wondered, that the vast, resurrected felon had never really been – had been but a figment of his mind ... a consequence, maybe, of Mrs Hardcastle's heavy cooking? For certainly, the events of the previous four and twenty hours – as he remembered them – had been of an unusual, even striking cast.

Abruptly he shook his head. If there had been no Black Jack, how come he was on the road to Ewell with a bounding lunatic at his side?

None the less, he continued to toy with the notion of Black Jack's being his own private invention; in support of which he recalled a certain childhood dream of a man-of-war of which he was mysteriously the master. So real had it seemed that, when he'd waked early, he'd rushed down to the harbour to

board it: and been much distressed to find it nowhere. Yet that proud, nodding vessel had been complete down to the tiniest detail of rust upon a cannon and a wart on the boatswain's cheek.

There was nothing to Black Jack, neither the specks of filth in his beard, nor the angry weal on his neck, nor his jagged forefingernail that was more detailed or believable – save his awesome contempt.

The lane which, at the outset, had been of no great consequence, was now sunk to a poor cart track. Sometimes it trickled under arched trees, then improved briefly to take in a sweep of landscape ... till once more it wandered into a green tunnel where twigs and branches, broke off by the passage of some loaded wagon, littered the shady ground.

Here Belle's unending chatter – by reason of the leafy confinement – grew too loud for even Tolly's dreaming quite to shut out. The sea of pity into which he'd fallen on first beholding her, began to evaporate. He discovered himself to be growing irritable – for Belle's talk was as tedious as an infant's. She was for ever demanding him to look at this and that – and at her own queer antics. Sometimes she skipped; sometimes she jumped – and sometimes she stuck a twig in her dusty hair – all for his unending admiration.

And worst of all, she seemed to have taken a strong fancy to him, making frequent attempts to give him a great moist kiss.

'For pity's sake, Belle,' muttered Tolly, his respectability much offended. 'Remember, you are a grown girl. You must do no such thing. *Please*, Belle –'

For a moment she'd looked abashed; and Tolly, seeing how poorly she *was* grown, would relent and hold out his hand. On which all would begin again ... till the boy realized Belle's infantile cunning was turning his remorse into a means of making fun of him.

He strode angrily ahead and the mad girl had to hop and leap to keep pace with him, chattering as inconsequentially as ever. Or almost so; every once in a while her words made an uncanny sense that chilled the boy with their aptness.

'Wouldn't it be a blessing if I was to do myself a mischief and come to a merciful end?' she prattled ... and held out an evil white toadstool that she'd plucked up from somewhere and had been hiding under her cloak. It was a Destroying Angel.

With a cry of fear, Tolly snatched it from her and flung it away. She did not seem to mind. Indeed, she seemed to forget the incident directly – such was her condition. Afterwards the boy wondered if he'd done the right thing. Would it not have been a sort of blessing if –?

He shook his head and wondered what his uncle, the sea-captain, would have said. Yet, despite the solemn cast of his thoughts, he could not stop from noticing that the mad girl's antics were afterwards a trifle subdued. He fancied that his own dread of the Destroying Angel had touched her in a clear place. He shivered on a sudden vague and nameless hope.

Then she had her strange vision again – of the black tower and the sun going to bed in a blanket. As before, it was followed by frantic screams and violence; but, mercifully, Tolly was ready this time. He was able to wrap her in her cloak, and he suffered no damage: but his hope was blown to the winds...

Presently the lane began to improve – as if it was smartening itself up for entry into Ewell. The trees diminished and, as the boy and the mad girl ambled on, the air grew quick with a cheerful hubbub. Then, on rounding a bend, they came upon a very agreeable sight.

A travelling fair had halted in a field outside the town. Some five or six gaudily painted wagons were drawn up in a half circle, like a huge tinsel jaw into which thronged a great company of purse-happy countryfolk with their fluttering children and bonneted wives.

There was a wagon that seemed to have exploded and burst its side to sell off – what looked in the bright April sun – to be the Crown Jewels of all the monarchs of the East. There was a wagon of Mystery, painted with stars and crescents and frantic comets, from which smoke was coming – as if one of the comets had accidentally gone off. There was a wagon of midgets (a shade on the large size): there was –

'Would you like to go to the Fair, Belle?' said Tolly, with a gentle indulgence that partly hid his own interest; he had five shillings from the first fallen coach on the Croydon road.

The mad girl stared uneasily towards the crowd that shifted and jiggled against the harbouring wagons like a high tide.

'If you hold my hand, Tolly. I'll go with you then.'

So they drifted off the road and across the field, encountering a strong smell of rum and burnt sugar.

Tolly bought two sausages from the wagon of Mystery, and a brass bangle from the wagon that was disposing of Crown

Jewels. They paid a penny to stare in the window of the midgets' wagon – the inside of which was got up like a dolls' house; but with furnishings on a grand scale even for a fully grown family, to set off the littleness of the midgets who were not so small as they might have been.

But there was one wagon that drew Tolly more powerfully than all the others; anxiously, Belle clung to him as he edged through the crowd that besieged it.

This wagon was neither gilded nor fantastic but of a plain blue with 'Dr Daniel Carmody' painted in bold white script on its side. And standing on a step at the back, in black coat, physician's wig and gentleman's mauve breeches, was Dr Carmody himself.

A short, neat built man with the most powerful and intelligent head Tolly had ever seen. Indeed, it might have belonged to a larger man altogether and come to Dr Carmody by mistake ... for it glanced down, from time to time, somewhat deprecatingly. But when it looked up there was a deep radiance and humanity in the eyes that no man could have opposed. He was selling – for a shilling a bottle – the Elixir of Youth.

Or, rather, was not selling it. Even arguing strongly against such a thing.

'No!' he shouted. 'This ain't a joke! This ain't to be taken lightly!'

A cheerful, speckle-faced young woman who was holding out a shilling and being prodded on by her companions, jeered loudly at the doctor for a mean fraud.

'Oh, my child!' bellowed back the doctor, staring down with an extra touch of radiance and humanity. 'Don't meddle with this! 'Tis for the old, the wrinkled, the bent, the aching in limb and spirit! 'Tis to make them as – as little children. 'Tis to give them back that strength in 'appiness that I see is so powerful in you. 'Tis to give them back their innocence – that I see is strong in you!'

Here there was a burst of gaudy laughter which distressed

the doctor – for he frowned and held up his hand reproach-fully. 'Her soul is innocent, my friends. Her heart is simple. She is now what I would 'ave the aged and the bitter become. *This* is for *them!*' (He held aloft the bottle – of which a goodly number could be seen, stowed in the wagon.) 'God knows what mischief it would wreck on 'er constitution – which is now so soft and pliable!' (Cries of 'Here, here!' and, 'Yes, indeed!') 'For part of its strength,' went on the doctor earnestly, 'lies in its strange power to dissolve the 'orny mesentery, the chalky membrane, so to speak, of constitutions grown hard with loneliness and time. With no such hardness to melt – God knows 'ow it would act! No! You shan't have it, my child! Not for ten thousand shillings!'

Defiantly, the doctor shook the bottle at his audience, as if it were a sword.

Now in the forefront of the crowd, not far from the speckle-faced young woman, was a lady on whom the doctor's words seemed to have a sombre effect. She had not yet come to middle age, yet her spirit seemed already bent-backed. Though she wore sprigged muslin stretched over a gay hoop, there was little of gaiety in her eyes, in the lines about her mouth, or in the furrows of her brow. She gazed up at Dr Carmody and his bottle with a bitterness and a regret that not all her bright complexion could veil. She shook her head – and sighed. She pressed her worn fingers into the arm of her sharp-faced son: a lad of Tolly's age, give or take a year.

But she did not notice – as Tolly did – that her boy was grown restless. For he took her entirely by surprise.

And not her alone – but Dr Carmody, likewise. Perhaps his intention was no more than a sudden comic humour: perhaps it was deeper and sprang, in part, from a concern for his melancholy mother, doubtless a widow . . .

He broke free and snatched the bottle Dr Carmody was unluckily brandishing.

Shrieks came up from the crowd – and laughter, too. Belle trembled with fright and clung to Tolly fiercely.

'Dick! Dick!' screamed the fearful mother.

'Boy! Boy! Come back!' shouted the doctor, pale with alarm. 'You'll harm yourself!'

Now began a terrific succession of spoutings up in the crowd as the fugitive boy darted hither and thither among cloying gowns and stout legs: popping into the air unexpectedly with a shout and a grin and a wave of the deadly bottle.

'Don't drink it! Don't – don't, boy!' roared the doctor.

Too late. The boy, finding himself trapped, grew angry with fright. 'Old fool!' he shouted wildly and, uncorking the bottle, gulped the liquid down.

At once the crowd shrank back from him, formed an uneasy circle ... fearfully interested – as if he was about to blow up with a venomous roar ...

The boy had dropped the bottle. He began to grin stupidly. He licked his lips. Then, of a horrible sudden, he clutched first his belly then his head and began to whimper and groan in a pitiful fashion. He seemed to be trying to speak. But could not. Could not anyhow. Eerie mewings came out of him, when at last he managed to utter one terrible cry of, 'Mama!'

Then he plunged, weeping, into the crowd and was lost from sight.

An instant later it seemed – though it must have been longer – there came a shriek and a cascade of frantic, disbelieving laughter. It was the mother.

'Oh my God! Oh my God! Look! Look!'

From under her gay muslin skirts crept a bundle of clothing that had been her son's. Everyone recognized it: there was no doubt. Within this bundle – in its crumpled heart – mewing and dribbling and squealing, was an infant of no more than twelve months! Dr Carmody's Elizir had done its business too well.

Demented, the mother seized up her transformed child – her laughter now gone into deep and helpless sobs.

'I – I warned him, ma'am,' groaned the wretched doctor, his large head bowed in guilty grief. He turned to the amazed crowd – a few of whom were still grinning, but not with much amusement. 'I warned him. You all heard me ... you'll bear witness ... I gave him fair warning. I knew when I made it that this powerful substance would bring someone to disaster!'

'Disaster?' screamed the mother violently. 'Yes – there'll be disaster for you! I'll go to the Justice! I'll have you taken for this! I'll see you hanged for what you done!'

'But, madam –' cried the ruined doctor.

'Oh God, God – what's he done to a poor widow?'

'But, madam –'

'And he was a well-grown lad ... fine, straight legs ... a clear eye and a cheek like a – a butterfly.' She broke off into sobs and attempted to calm the infant which had begun to bawl as if in a dim memory of what it once had been. 'Never a pock mark on him.' She was pushing her way out of the crowd. 'And now – and now – look! I must go through it all again! And – and he weren't an easy infant ever! Oh, as Heaven's my witness, I'll see you punished, Doctor Carmody!'

Last seen, she was hurrying across the meadow in the direction of Ewell and justice, with the pitiful evidence clutched whining in her arms.

Hastily Dr Carmody began to pack up his wagon.

'Forgive me, friends ... forgive me – but I must begone. My dear sir – madam, consider how little time I may have! Really, dear lady – and you, sir – and you! Take pity on my plight! So little time. Oh, ma'am, *please*! Would you all see me gaoled, then?'

In the midst of his hasty packing, first one, then another, then a dozen or more of the crowd pushed forward with their shillings – regardless of the doctor's urgency to be gone.

They were hard-looking, were these country folk, and selfish in their desires. Though they grinned sheepishly at one another and shrugged their worthy shoulders, there was, at back of it all, a piteous hope. Mostly they were in middle life, but there was a fair sprinkling of the morose and elderly, the bent and the infirm, the lonely and the sad to whom the chance of gain-ing once more the innocence of children was well worth the risk of a shilling.

So what could the luckless doctor do? He sold and sold and sold, watching most painfully the while for the approach of constables. Hurriedly, desperately, wildly he sold – as if he knew that, until all his stock was gone, the greedy crowd would never let him go.

'Buy one for me, Tolly,' begged mad Belle.

Tolly stared sadly at her. 'You're young enough, Belle. Your spirit couldn't stand getting any younger. Another step back and I don't think you'd be here at all.'

Presently the last of the bottles was gone and Dr Carmody mopped his striking brow. The constables were not come yet. He turned to Tolly and Belle who were now alone by the wagon – the crowd having melted off, not wanting to be caught up in the proceedings.

'Go, go!' he muttered. 'I've nothing now. Nothing – nothing!'

Tolly said softly, 'We – I only wanted to ask you something, sir. God forbid I'd want your mixture – for *her*.' He nodded his head at Belle, who smiled radiantly and began to pick her nose.

The doctor glanced involuntarily at the girl – then shrugged his shoulders; which action his fine head seemed somehow to disapprove of.

'I thought,' went on Tolly hesitantly, 'that you might have something – know of something that would help her. You see, she's daft as a mackerel, sir. She's mad –'

And he went on quickly to describe Belle's malady and as much of his own plight as he thought necessary.

'The poor thing,' mused Dr Carmody, looking with great humanity at the lunatic, who smiled with recognition at the familiar name. 'A natural, eh? A soul locked in primaeval innocence, so to speak. Shut up behind bars of unmeaning laughter. My dear young man, where are you taking her?'

'South, sir. To the sea. To my uncle, who's a sea-captain in

Lancing, and vastly experienced in all manner of things. He's my only hope.'

The doctor frowned. 'The case interests me, young man. If you'd care to come up on the wagon with me, we'll talk as we go, eh?'

So Tolly and Belle climbed up on the front of the blue wagon while the doctor harnessed up his horse. Presently they were away, rumbling through Ewell and on towards Epsom and Ashstead.

Contrary to his promise, the doctor said nothing as they travelled. He was busily watching the road as if constables were likely to come up like knapweed in the tall grass ... When they'd gone about a mile, he pulled up and whistled softly.

Almost at once there rose up from a ditch on the left of the road, first the bereaved mother – infant in her arms – and then, whole, well-grown, cheeks like butterflies, her sharp-faced son!

'Mrs Carmody and daughter, young man: and me apprentice, Hatch. Ah! One's driven to queer lengths to make a living these days!'

Speechless with amazement, anger and deep disappointment, Tolly stared down at the fraudulent little family – and then the sharp-faced boy looked up. The two apprentices took an immediate dislike to one another.

'What madness is this?' cried Mrs Carmody, scowling furiously at Tolly and Belle. 'D'you want us all in gaol, Dr Carmody?'

'You're mistook, dear – quite mistook!' said the doctor, gaily. 'They're a pair of 'elpless, 'apless innocents – only just 'atched, in a manner of speaking. She's a natural, my dear. A simple ... an idiot, y'know –'

'– Like yourself, Dr Carmody!'

'Peace, ma'am!' said the doctor, his magnificent head looking more out of place than ever. 'There's possibilities in the lunatic! Don't you see 'em? I'd have thought the girl I married would have seen 'em straight off! Such innocence! Such childlike bliss! What material, ma'am! What a heaven-sent sample! 'Tis my chance, ma'am, to prove my – um – my genius, so to speak! Oh, Mrs Carmody, for pity's sake don't stand in me way!'

The dispute ran on for some minutes, brief upon the lady's side, but long and persevering on the doctor's ... while the two apprentices fed their dislikes by staring at one another.

'And who will feed her?'

'I will, of course, Mrs Carmody. Was there ever any question of it?'

Mrs Carmody was weakening, and the doctor went from strength to strength ...

Abruptly, now, he turned to Tolly – in whom, perhaps, he read some bitterness and uncertainty. Little lamps seemed to be lit behind his eyes, lending his large, wise face a more than ordinary radiance.

'My boy,' he said gently, 'do not be disheartened by our little pretence. The money we gain by it is for a good cause. 'Tis all for my studies into the mortal soul – the spirit – the mind. 'Tis a great adventure, my dear. A voyage of exploring. And, like a careful captain, I must needs take on merchandise to sell to heathens to pay for the cost of the voyage.'

Touched in a deep part of his heart, Tolly nodded – and the good doctor went on, filling the boy with dreams and the odd scraps of knowledge picked up in a lifetime of fraud.

Once more, vague hopes began to flicker in Tolly's heart, and he kept glancing to the wretched, dusty, ill-grown Belle, who had begun to dribble down the front of her cloak.

'And we are going into Sussex, my boy. We are travelling south, like you – towards the sea. The opportunity is enormous: on both sides. Oh, what mysteries we may – together – unlock in her remarkable mind! Oh, what secrets of original bliss –'

'Do you see it, Tolly?' muttered Belle of a sudden, peering into the inside of the wagon.

'What, Belle?'

'A tall black tower, topped with gold. White angels with white wings fly about it. And – and all the world's singing a lullaby, for the sun's gone to bed in a blanket...'

'My child,' said the doctor kindly. ''Tis in your poor mind. There's no such thing. There –'

She flew at him with screams and shrieks and all but knocked him from the wagon, till Tolly secured her. Then her shriekings seemed doubled as she fought. The Carmodys' infant awoke and promptly added its screams to Belle's; most likely imagining itself come upon a conversation in a language that, for once, it had some command of.

The sounds produced by the infant and the idiot were of a wild and despairing nature – as if what they had to say to each other was far from comforting. Mrs Carmody vigorously rocked her daughter back and forth to stop its noise, while the doctor, stopping up his ears with his fingers, was fascinated beyond measure.

'My dear young man – you cannot take her with you! The danger of it! Have you considered? What a burden – what a responsibility – what a fearsome risk! You must come with us! Your only chance. We, at least, can protect you. With us you'll be safe...'

Even as he spoke, Belle grew quiet again and Tolly let her go. Her face was back in nearly all its bland contentment; though Tolly fancied it to be a little veiled. The doctor took his fingers out of his ears and, with warm and honest concern, impressed yet again on Tolly the hugeness of the burden he seemed to have taken on.

'A heavy task, young man. Heavy – heavy...'

Tolly looked at skinny, wispy Belle, and gave a rueful smile. She was not so heavy as all that.

Suddenly the sharp-faced apprentice – who, all the while, had been looking unusually crafty – shouted: 'They're coming, master! Here they come!'

The remaining wagons of the little fair were rocking and bumping into view.

'Splendid people!' said Dr Carmody, waving to them. 'A little world, young man. A world of innocence and kindness for you and your – your lunatic. Here you may be safe from the shocks and whirlwinds and spiritual earthquakes that roam and crack and roar outside.'

The leading wagon belonged to the midgets and, as it came to a halt, two of that little company climbed down and ran excitedly to Dr Carmody.

'Daniel! Daniel Carmody! Our fortune's made! Come see what we've got! A treasure! Look in our window and see! Don't we look tiny? Quite ant-like! The contrast, Daniel! The striking contrast of it!'

Dr Carmody, Mrs Carmody and sharp-faced Hatch all went to look; and came back, awed into silence. Then it was Tolly's turn.

He peered in at the midgets' window where all was pathetically oversize. He went white. He groaned in amazement and dread.

Looking out at him, with huge and uncanny malevolence, was the face of Black Jack!

'Did you think you'd shook me off, Tolly? Did you fancy you'd lost me? Set your heart at rest, Tolly. You was never out of my sight. That lunatic's worth ten pound, Tolly; and I'm going to have it!'

He peered at the boy in mock dismay. 'What's amiss, Tolly? Why so pale? Are you frightened? It wasn't in your mind to cheat poor Black Jack? Not Black Jack what you resurrected from the dead?'

Then he laughed – and the wagon shook like a ship in a storm . .

6

THE caravan of wagons moved like a mighty painted *Argosy* down the narrow Surrey lanes. It clanked and jingled and rumbled and heaved at a slow pace ... no faster than the running feet of cottage children who bore it company, waving and shouting by the hedgerows like ragged sprites – till distant voices called them home.

The order of the wagons was thus: forward, making the prow, so to speak, rolled the Carmodys; then came the midgets; amidships moved the wagon of Mystery (commanded by a mysterious Mr Arbuthnot and his still more mysterious wife); next came a nondescript wagon that had once got itself entangled with the caravan and had never managed to break free; then last of all, forming the poop or afterworks of this jointed vessel, lumbered the wagon of bangles, kettles and all the Crown Jewels of the East.

If there was a Captain, it was Dr Carmody; though Mrs Arbuthnot in the wagon of Mystery was always suspected of mutiny for she told fortunes and never allotted the doctor a prosperous one.

'A dark man will cross your path at Basingstoke,' was her latest, during a brief halt. 'And so long as you continue to put yourself first, Doctor Carmody, you'll bring all to confusion. You have been warned!'

The doctor beamed vaguely, but Tolly Dorking was chilled to the bottom of his soul. Too well he guessed who the dark man might be; too well he could imagine the confusion ... of bone and blood and frightened brains spilled out by the raging Black Jack.

He peered sideways at the doctor's profile which was bright with hope and promise as he leaned forward in an urging manner over his horse's wobbling rump.

Should he warn Dr Carmody of what was directly behind? He shuddered and shook his head on the thought of what might follow. For who, aboard the wagons, could confine Black Jack in the full flood of his health and strength?

Such fears as this continued to plague him till the end of the day's journeying, when the wagons turned off the road and into a field where they were to stay the night.

An iron cage was fetched out of the nondescript wagon and a fire was kindled in it, growing lively as the air turned dark and still – till the circling wagons seemed to jig gently in and out of their own shadows, like gilded, scarlet dreams ... The *Argosy* was at anchor.

Those for whom there was room, slept in their wagons. The others rolled themselves into blankets and slept wherever the ground was kind. Belle was within. Tolly slept outside.

Or, more exactly, lay entangled in his blanket, staring towards the fire which was watched over by the owner of the nondescript wagon, doubtless dreaming of where he might go and what he might do when at last he should escape.

Tolly turned on his back and looked up to the sky. He cried out.

It was gone. In its place was Black Jack.

Not the smallest sound had betrayed his coming. Huge strength and huge stealth: formidable combination. Tolly groaned at the hopelessness of his situation. Against the terrible man who reared above him, what could he offer?

Black Jack raised his ragged forefinger to his lips, and squatted down beside the unhappy draper's apprentice. Tolly eyed his unpleasant hand.

'The – the coach? What ... became of it?'

Black Jack's eyes glimmered in the firelight. He rubbed his neck – then shook his head, as if there was something that troubled him.

'That's my affair.'

'Did you ... murder?'

A look of cunning came into Black Jack's face. He shook his head again.

'They've gone their ways. But I know where. So you and me, Tolly, will soon be calling on 'em for that ten pounds.'

Silently Tolly thanked God that they'd gone somewhere where they still had dominion over ten pounds, and so were still on the earth and not under it. For the thought of their deaths at Black Jack's resurrected hands had haunted Tolly powerfully.

But whatever relief he'd been afforded by the ruffian's mysterious magnanimity was quite cancelled now.

'The lunatic,' grunted Black Jack. 'She's for a private madhouse. And that's where she's going, Tolly. Dead or alive – take your pick – that mad thing's worth ten pound.'

Tolly glanced up at the dark wagon in which the ten pound idiot was asleep.

'Must we – must we take her, Mister Jack?'

Slowly, and with menace, Black Jack nodded. A pang of distress invaded Tolly's heart. Not that he knew much about private madhouses – his uncle, the sea-captain, never having spoken of them – but he suspected them of being dark, cruel places where wispy things like Belle would quickly wither and die.

Now sounds among the wagons disturbed the conversation. The watch by the fire was being changed. Round-backed Mr Arbuthnot had come out of the wagon of Mystery like a black half-moon in high boots and cape, and was arranging himself for his portion of the night. He shivered and poked fresh wood into the iron cage; and the fire leaped and crackled and sent up a fountain of smoking sparks. Here and there the shapes of sleepers stirred and mumbled; a horse sighed noisily . . . Then, as if to undo his disturbance of the night, Mr Arbuthnot began to hum and sing softly, to lull the anchored *Argosy* back into the quieter depths of sleep.

> 'There was an old woman tossed up in a basket
> Seventeen times as high as the moon ...'

Involuntarily the boy and the giant looked up, but saw no such queer portent. Indeed, the Carmody's wagon creaked a little, and from within came the familiar sound of dusty coughing.

'Give her a draught,' mumbled Mrs Carmody. 'Give her a syrup, Doctor – before she wakes the babe. Dear God! Hearken to her now!'

Belle had given over coughing and had begun to sing. A hoarse and unwholesome sound. The old song seemed to have set off some trifle of memory –

> 'Where she was going, I couldn't but ask it
> For in her hand she carried a – a chopper –'

'Broom!' said Mrs Carmody irritably. 'Broom – broom! She carried a broom! Dear Lord above! What would she do with a chopper? Doctor Carmody! D'you hear? A chopper! Your precious idiot has notions of murder! She'll savage us in our beds! That's what you'll have done – killed us!'

'Peace, ma'am,' mumbled the doctor. 'You'll wake Cassandra –'

'Cassandra! What a tomfool name to give a tiny babe! What a tomfool man you are! Well – this'll be your end, Doctor Carmody ... if it's any consolation to us who'll be dead! She'll do for you. That elegant head of yours won't look so grand when it's off at the neck!'

'Peace, ma'am. The idiot ain't doing any harm ... the innocence of children –'

> 'Where are you going to, up so high?
> To eat up the cobwebs out of the sky –'

Belle went on uncertainly following the musical Mr Arbuthnot. Then she coughed again and stopped singing. In a little while the Carmodys' wagon sank back into a drowsy silence.

Tolly sighed and looked to the relentless Black Jack. He

stared. The huge man had retreated some yards. His eyes glittered.

'That was her – eh?' he muttered. 'That was the lunatic?'

Of a sudden, Tolly suspected a strange thing. He suspected that this mighty ruffian, this vast, murdering felon who feared neither God nor the Devil nor even the hangman, was struck with dread by skinny, mad Belle!

A weakness! Heaven be thanked – he had a weakness!

Black Jack was biting on his lip and staring at the wagon. Sweat stood out on his brow – which the firelight turned to a likeness of beaded blood.

Now the boy knew for certain. The monster was afraid. At once the reason for Black Jack's stealthy following stood clear. Not for worlds would he have walked beside the pair of them. Madness appalled him!

A great relief filled Tolly's heart. So long as he lived, so long as he bore her company, he, Tolly Dorking, stood between the idiot and the giant with harsh intent.

He must have smiled or shown some other unlucky sign of confidence, for Black Jack clenched his fists menacingly.

'You'll not go against me, Tolly. I'll smash you, else –'

'And I'll not go with you. Neither me nor her. You'll not have her for the madhouse; for ten pound or ten thousand, Black Jack!'

Black Jack scowled at him in furious disbelief.

'She's infected you! You've gone as mad as her! What would you want with a lunatic instead of ten pound?'

Suddenly he unclenched his fists. A look of concern came over his enormous face.

'She'll strangle you, Tolly. She'll bite through your neck one black night. Wouldn't want that to happen, would we?'

'She's only a poor, skinny, dusty thing, Black Jack. She's no more strength than a mouse –'

'Strength?' whispered Black Jack, with a shiver. 'What does a puny little weasel like you know about strength? I'm strong. In me full 'ealth an' strength I could kill a bear. But . . .'

He fell silent. The natural harshness of his features took on that look of stony dread Tolly had first seen upon them when he'd lain in his coffin.

'But . . . what, Black Jack?'

'But if you don't fetch her forth when I tells you,' said Black Jack, coming to himself, 'I swear by this stinking world I'll pound you to mud, Tolly. To a lump of bleeding mud. And where will that uncanny mite be then?'

But now there were more movings among the wagons as Mrs Arbuthnot came out with something in a pot for her watchful spouse. The firelight danced among the strands of her high-blown hair so that she, like the heavenly bodies on her wagon, seemed briefly in a state of fiery explosion.

Then she became a shadow beside her shadowy husband as she sat with him awhile and, in a low voice, confided mysteries . . .

'For pity's sake, Black Jack,' muttered Tolly, turning back to the bulky ruffian.

But Black Jack had gone. As silently as he'd come, he vanished into the unsteady shadows. For a long time Tolly stared at them, fancying each was the giant, crouching down and watching him: for he felt eyes upon him . . . invisible, menacing eyes that never faltered or closed up in human sleep.

By the fire the Arbuthnots had fallen silent. Then Mrs Arbuthnot rustled back to her wagon and once more her husband began to sing.

And yet Tolly stared – for the feeling of being watched was still strong.

Then, little by little, sleep got the better of him and his hopes and fears drifted off behind a dozing curtain – like actors, to reappear in the strange and gaudy costumes of dreams . . .

The watchful eyes blinked sharply. They had seen much. Likewise a pair of ears – belonging to the same – had heard much.

Hatch, the doctor's apprentice, sat up. He looked about him, marking well the landscape of the night – the disposition of the sleepers and the passages through the shadows.

With deep interest he'd seen which way the giant had gone. He glanced back to Tolly, waited maybe for half a minute more, then, like a fox or a stoat, crept off in Black Jack's wake.

As he moved, the firelight touched the edge of his face. The expression thereon would have been humorous, had it not been vicious; it would have been hopeful, had it not been strained with greed.

If he met with Black Jack among the shadows, no sound of their conversing was heard. But it was more than an hour before he returned; and to the previous qualities in his face was now added another – which would have been cheerful, had it not been cruel.

Still at his watch, Mr Arbuthnot came to the end of his song.

> 'Shall I go with thee?
> Aye – by and by.'

Hatch stared at the Carmodys' wagon – then back to the shadows he'd left. Slowly, he grinned . . .

7

THURSDAY'S dawn was grey of face. Very heavy and tearful was the sky that looked down – as if it was much oppressed by what it saw. The last watcher by the dying fire – the proprietor of the Eastern Jewels (a shabby, wizened tinker) – prepared to go, for his time was up.

And not a moment too soon. Unable to hold back its tears, the sky abandoned itself to grief. At about a quarter to six it began to rain.

The fire hissed, spat and finally gave up the ghost in the shape of a frail wisp of smoke, when the Crown Jeweller returned to his wagon and his dozing wife (who jingled faintly with bracelets she'd been unable to get off).

The outside sleepers, touched with wet, awoke, hatched grumpily out of their blankets and crawled for shelter.

But Tolly never moved. Having been long in dropping asleep, he was still fathoms deep in it. Neither the gentle spotting of the rain nor the light of morning reached down to him. Wherever he was, it must have been in a pleasant and hopeful place. He smiled blindly into his blanket as if there was no such thing as Black Jack or the poor mad thing who clung about his heart.

Even the chief cause of his remaining so long awake – the feeling of being watched from the shadows – did not trouble his dreaming.

Which was a mercy. This watching had been sharp, unfriendly and shrewd. And it still was.

Now the rain grew brisker and began to rattle on the wagons' roofs. Tolly began to stir and struggle as if preparing to swim.

'Haul in the topsail!' he shouted. 'The yard's adrift! We sink – we sink –'

He sat up. Bewildered, he stared at the torn grass and rain-prickled mud on which the painted *Argosy* had struck and run aground.

Then he recollected his circumstance. Cautiously he peered about for sight of Black Jack. He feared that the passage of night might have sealed up the monster's only weakness, and that he'd be coming on – madness notwithstanding.

Black Jack was not to be seen. Yet he could not rid himself of the sense of being watched. But from where? No living thing was in sight.

The fire lay dead in its cage, and the wagons humped glumly around it. Very sad and draggled they looked, with their glamorous gildings all streaked with tears of rain. The wagon of Mystery – with its comets and stars and crescent moons – seemed no more than the forgotten dream of some child, long since grown up and maybe dead as well.

Nor was Dr Daniel Carmody's wagon a more hopeful sight. His very name, painted on the side, seemed in imminent danger of being washed away.

Tolly sighed and crept out of his sodden blanket. As he did so he wondered fleetingly if the invisible eyes upon him could have been Belle's; for it seemed of a sudden that it was from the Carmodys' wagon that the watching came.

Yet when he thumped respectfully on the wagon's side and called: 'It's Tolly Dorking here! And wet as a mackerel!' it was not Belle who answered.

Instead, there were rapid sounds of objects slipping and falling; then Dr Carmody's head poked out of the flap that served as the door.

Directly Tolly's gloom lifted. He'd forgotten the inspiration of the doctor's countenance; and now the second sight of it quite cancelled out the discomfort of the wet.

'Come inside, young man!' invited the doctor, and opened the flap wide enough for Tolly to catch a glimpse of tumbled bed linen, nightgowns and quick bare feet as Mrs Carmody, taken unawares, bolted behind a curtain that divided the wagon, front from rear.

'Is Belle –?' began Tolly, and the doctor winked and said: 'Sleeping like a blessed babe, my boy! Idiots, you know, have remarkable capacities . . . much to learn . . . great mysteries . . . deeps unplumbed . . . yes, indeed . . . Call you Tolly?'

These gaps in the doctor's talk, popping up between so that he seemed to converse in archipelagos, so to speak, were not of his own making; for he was the most continuous of men. The cause was Mrs Carmody, who, in her hasty dressing behind the curtain, had trod on Cassandra and precipitated a terrified howling that was broken only by a need to draw new breath. It was in the intervals so formed that the doctor was heard.

Then the idiot Belle woke up and, finding herself in uncanny surroundings and believing herself to have been lost beyond recovery, began to shriek, 'Tolly! Tolly!' with the utmost desperation.

'I'm here, Belle!' roared Tolly eagerly. 'You're safe and sound! I'm here – I'm here!' And into the wagon he climbed while Dr Carmody shrugged his shoulders and closed the flap to shut out the dreadful weather.

(But even in his haste of entering, Tolly wondered again who could have been watching him from the Carmodys' wagon – for he was tolerably certain the scrutiny had come from here.)

The dim interior of Dr Carmody's home was strong with the sweet and sour smells of idiots, babes and warm sleep, and the uproar that had come out of it was but a whisper to the pandemonium within.

The doctor, who had sat or fallen upon a basket, continued to discourse wisely and gently – but in islands that lay farther and farther apart. Belle, hearing Tolly come up, had grown violently agitated and was making strong attempts to get at him; but was being prevented by Mrs Carmody, who'd a great sense of decency and was attempting to dress her first.

'Naked as a badger!' she kept shouting as the curtain shook and billowed. 'She's naked as a badger – the shameless trollop! Come back here, miss!'

On which Belle shrieked, 'Tolly! Tolly! No! I won't wear green! He don't like me in green!'

'What's it matter what you wear?'

'Tolly – Tolly!'

Then, briefly, the idiot's alarmed face – or sometimes her skinny arm – would appear round the curtain, only to vanish directly as she was seized from behind.

'Brassy slut –'

'Not that one! He don't like it! Tolly –'

'The horny mesentery,' said the doctor, shaking his forefinger at Tolly; and his head went up and down rapidly as his voice vanished under the riotous tide beyond the curtain ... only to reappear, several miles farther off with, 'Twelve bottles for one and nine!'

'Upset her basket!' raged Mrs Carmody. 'Tipped it out like –'

'– Two eggs in sugar!' put in Dr Carmody – then vanished again.

'Rummaging like a mole!'

'Tolly – Tolly! My shawl's gone! My pretty lace shawl! And it suited –'

'It never was! Out of your mind! No lace shawl was ever there! What next, miss?'

'My muslin – my sprigged muslin! It's gone! He'd have liked it –'

'Grappling irons,' remarked Dr Carmody deeply.

'The red sash! It's gone – gone!'

Now the infant Cassandra, feeling herself to be neglected, provoked Mrs Carmody to further distraction by being sick. On which, the lucky aptness, Dr Carmody rose up with, 'Pickled herrings!' and went down again.

Then, like a cruel rock in the mist of this tumultuous sea,

Belle let out a scream of fury and despair. A terrible scream: a desolate, bewildered scream that silenced all but the ceaseless rain.

'Look! Look! They're being eaten! All my clothes! All – all!'

'Belle!' shouted Tolly – and plunged through the curtains.

In the midst of a storm of sheets, gowns and ruptured baskets, crouched the skinny, naked Belle. She was clutching the tail end of a brown dress, or pelisse. The rest of it was through the floorboards, being inexorably swallowed down.

'Tolly – Tolly!' howled Belle, in such a panic as only the mad can know. 'See! They're being eaten! What place is this you've brought me to? What have you done with your poor thing?'

'Slut!' shouted Mrs Carmody – and sought to cover the demented Belle (whose pale skin seemed scarce sufficient, so tight was it over her bones) with her skirts against the eyes of the intruder.

But Tolly's eyes were not for Belle. They were for the vanishing cloth. Not being mad, like Belle, he divined the cause. No grand consuming wagon for him. There was somebody underneath!

Soft hearts are easily combustible; and when they take fire, they burn with a sudden blaze. Thus gentle Tolly, when he saw the thin and dusty idiot crouching frantic over her departing finery, clutching at its last remnants in a desolate bewilderment, was consumed with a terrible rage.

He plunged from the wagon and rolled in the mud beneath. Slung between fore and aft axles hung something like a long, dropped belly. A hammock. Inside it lay the owner of the ever watchful eyes. And of more: a long hook, fashioned out of bent wire, and even now half through a gap in the floorboards and drawing down its latest catch.

It was Hatch – absorbed, ambitious and devious Hatch. Too late he saw the furious Tolly. Anxiously he yelled for Tolly to

keep off him – else he'd knife him, split his guts, slice his lousy throat.

But Tolly had a hold on his hair and was dragging him out into the filth and rain.

So they began to fight: Tolly in a fiery heat – and Hatch in a chilly desire to quench that heat for ever – and begone. His knife, his neat little knife! If only he could get it out!

Now they'd rolled clear of the wagon in an intricate engagement of thumping and kicking and biting that fairly boiled up the mud in their wake.

Over and over they went, making harsh sounds in each other's fierce faces, while the rain beat down on whoever was uppermost, plucking little silver spears out of his back.

Heads appeared out of wagon doors and windows. The Crown Jeweller's wife, half-made tiara tipsily over her ear, watched agape on the outcome; Mrs Arbuthnot, peering through curtains, doubtless knew it, but wanted to make sure ... while the Carmodys, proprietors of the scene, looked on quite stricken with amazement by the power of the double creature that jerked and strained and muttered in the mud.

But Belle – mad Belle – wrapped in a sheet, had an idiot rapture in her eyes. Her lips were parted and her breath came quick. Smiles and frowns chased each other over her pinched face as Tolly rolled above, below, then up again in passing triumph. Never was knight more wildly watched – by lady quite so strange.

'Tolly!' she cried; and Tolly, looking up, gave Hatch the brief advantage he desired. His knife was out. Tolly saw it – felt it urge his side. One more overturning and it would be in ...

Hatch spat in his face and began to heave.

'Tolly!' shrieked Belle – and Tolly, commending himself to the care of whoever would have him, clouted Hatch's head with his own.

Hatch screeched – fancying the wagon of Mystery, complete with exploding planets and stars, had fallen on him. Then they passed and he saw above him, bloody and tooth-chopped, Tolly's face.

Near senseless with pain, and doubtless still seeing the same dancing points of light that had astonished Hatch – for the eyes were shining – it still contrived to smile. Hatch had lost his knife.

Of a sudden Hatch saw Tolly's proud and happy face whisk up into the air and vanish!

'Leave him be!' snarled Black Jack as he twitched Tolly into the air and flung him a dozen feet away. 'He's a friend of mine!'

The battle was ended. Black Jack, who'd come out of the midgets' wagon, vast and dark as Fate, had stopped it. Now, with scarce a backward look, he shambled back again.

Tolly stared after him with all the bitterness of one from whom triumph has been unjustly snatched. In that moment he hated Black Jack with all of his heart and most of his soul.

He staggered upright, then trudged painfully to the Carmodys' wagon. So battered in body and mind was he, that he scarce noticed his enemy was gone: had limped off the field and vanished into the teeming rain.

He bent to pick up Belle's trampled belongings; attempted to brush the filth off of them – but added more. Then he went to her and offered up the spoils of his almost victory.

Never was knight more wet and draggled – nor never was lady more deeply pleased.

The idiot clapped her hands and tears of pride ran down her cheeks.

'Tolly – Tolly! Was it for me?'

'It was only a thief, Belle. A thief. Nothing worse. You're safe, now. Here, your dresses . . .'

She took them from him and, with a defiant look at Mrs Carmody, retired into the wagon to fondle her injured treasures and dream on her battered champion.

Yet all was not quite joyful with her. Her fine lace shawl

was gone; and not all of everyone's persuading could convince her that it had been but a shawl of the mind, a lace imagining, a piece of finery that had been spun on no other shuttles than those of her unfastened mind.

'This I count a grave symptom,' said Dr Carmody sombrely. 'Of a piece with her vision of the tower and the sun. Though all is not lost, dear Tolly, all is decidedly not well.'

Tolly bit his lip. No less than his limbs, his heart ached too. The mad girl was in it, crying for help.

'Can we not . . . make her happy, at least?'

The doctor gazed at him. His eyes shone. Tolly looked into them with renewed hope. There was something in their light that seemed to be speaking to him: if only he knew the language . . .

At eleven o'clock that morning the rain gave over and the sun came out. The *Argosy* grew busy and prepared to hoist anchor. Horses were fetched and harnessed. Tolly helped with Striker, the Carmodys' portly gelding, for Hatch was not come back.

Now all was stowed aboard, ropes were made fast and canvas latched secure. All was ready to move. Southward, had said the doctor: southward into Sussex. But still his apprentice was missing.

'Was he honest, I'd say he's gone for good,' declared Mrs Carmody, peering at the empty hammock and prodding it. 'But wherever that sharp, wicked little schemer's gone, it'll be for bad. I never liked him, Carmody. And it was hurtful to pretend he was my son.'

By noon the wagons were on the road. The Carmodys formed the prow and the aspiring Arbuthnots were amidships – having been outwitted once more by the superior skill and judgement of Mrs Carmody. The doctor took Tolly by the arm. He drew him to one side with a discreet smile.

'My dear young man – your chance has come! Opportunity

has knocked. Dare I say, thundered? Let it in, my boy! Let it in!'

Tolly stared at him wonderingly. The doctor held his hands to his splendid head and rocked it to and fro – as if to settle out some striking tumult within.

'A vacancy! Ain't I got a vacancy?'

Tolly put down the unworthy thought that the vacancy might be in what the doctor was holding, and waited.

'An apprenticeship such as no money could purchase nor no articles define. It's yours, my boy! Yours! What a chance for you! I'll teach you all I know. Everything! Then together, dear boy – together we'll go through this dark old world and hang a little tinsel on every tree! Hand in hand, my boy!'

He clasped his hands together, and Tolly wondered if he'd a third one somewhere, his visible pair being mutually occupied.

'The crowning profession – and you'll be the brightest jewel in it! God's will! It was God's will that sent you to me ... you and your piteous idiot! Ha – ha!'

The doctor couldn't refrain from laughing softly with delight at the prospect before them.

Much bewildered, much in doubt, Tolly hesitated. He felt himself to be on the edge of a sea as wide and wild and yet as wonderful as any that lapped the Sussex shore.

If he set sail with the painted *Argosy*, what would he leave behind? His uncle, the sea-captain. His hopes of a respectable trade: for no one, with the best will in the world, could call Dr Carmody's trade respectable. Remarkable, maybe ... even exciting: but respectable, no. He shivered as he pictured his upright uncle learning of his nephew's new apprenticeship.

But the wind was blowing fair. Aboard the *Argosy* was the frail idiot whose eyes lit up when she saw him, and whose only defence against the dark madhouse was Tolly ...

'Will you, my boy?' the doctor was saying, his magnificent countenance on his meagre body looking more than ever as if he'd dined with angels and come away with the wrong head. 'Will you come aboard and sail to glory with me?'

Tolly nodded, and the doctor beamed with delight.

'Got him, Mrs C!' he shouted – then pointed down to the hammock.

'Yours. All yours. Rent-free, my boy!'

The doctor climbed up on his wagon, and extended his hand to his new apprentice. Tolly took it and heaved himself up.

But, as he did so, he glimpsed something that made him wonder sharply at the wisdom of his choice. He had seen the midgets' wagon. In its window was part of a huge and terrible face. Black Jack had been watching him intently. Tolly stared back with defiance. But the giant seemed unconcerned. His eyes shifted slightly. He stared past Tolly as if he'd ceased to exist. He stared into a great distance as if his strange wild heart was with another boy now; a boy who was arrowing north, perhaps to Islington, at his bidding . . .

8

MITCHELL, the coachman and Under-Keeper of Dr Jones's Madhouse, had had a fright. None the less, he discharged the last of his night's duties – which consisted in seeing all chains, locks and bolts were secure on the gentlemen's side – before he came, white-faced and trembling, down to the hallway.

Here, at nine o'clock each night, he would meet with Mrs Mitchell – matron, cook and Under-Keeper on the distaff side commodiously rolled into one – who would have discharged like duties among the ladies. Then, together, they would inform Dr Jones and Parson Hall in the front parlour that all was well or otherwise. After which they'd retire to their own quarters below stairs.

'Thank God you've come!' whispered Mitchell, as his wife appeared, lamp in hand and Register under her arm. 'I've seen a devil!'

'Whereabouts?' asked Mrs Mitchell, not wonderfully surprised. Ten years among the demented had enlarged her understanding of what a mortal man might see with his own starting eyes.

She was a stout person with a round face and a pelmet of faded white curls. Although she was firm and sometimes harsh, although she was apt to bully and shout, and to have favourites and enemies among her frantic charges, it was strongly suspected she'd a heart of gold. Or of some metal very like it.

'First floor window, Mrs Mitchell. That's where I saw it. Same room where them two brandy-merchants are chained.'

'Sure it wasn't one of *their* devils, Mitchell? From all accounts, they got enough and to spare.'

'I ain't up the chimney yet, Mrs Mitchell. The devil I saw was me own.'

'Who says you're indisposed, Mitchell? You're as entitled to see a goblin as any living soul in the establishment.'

For Mrs Mitchell was broad-minded enough to call no one mad. 'Why bless you!' she'd say of a comfortable evening, 'they're as sane as you and me. Poor souls – all they need is understanding. And discipline, of course. You can't stand no nonsense from 'em. Why, they'd cut your throat as soon as your back was turned!'

'There, Mrs Mitchell! There it is again!'

Mitchell was pointing a horny finger at the window at the head of the stairs. An apparition that might well have belonged elsewhere in the terrible house was staring in.

A foul and filthy face was pressed against the glass. Then, seeing itself observed, the semblance of a grin appeared, and its sharp, sharp eyes glittered like Judas windows in what seemed to be a mansion of mud.

'It's a boy, Mitchell,' said Mrs Mitchell softly. 'Most likely he's a thief. Go see if you can catch him, dear.'

Which proved to be surprisingly easy. Indeed, the boy was at the front door even as it was opened.

'Name of Hatch,' he said. 'To see Dr Jones.'

'What was you doing at the window?'

'Which one?' he grinned. 'I been climbing round 'em all. You got some interesting cases here, all right.'

'You've been spying,' said Mrs Mitchell, nodding to her husband to shut the door behind the boy.

'Spying, ma'am? Never! Just curious ... being in the same line meself. For you see, ma'am, I know of a case ... a poor thing what was lost out of a coach –'

Here Hatch fumbled in his coat and drew out a corner of spattered lace. 'Me Boney-Fridays, ma'am. 'Tis the poor thing's shawl. See! There's her name. "Carter", very nicely worked in pink. But we call her Belle. Belle Carter. Lost on Tuesday; found on Wednesday; and now it's Friday!'

'Go tell the doctor, Mitchell!' muttered his wife hurriedly. 'Tell him news has come!'

Mitchell departed and the sturdy lady beckoned Hatch towards a doorway on the left of the stairs.

'We can wait in here, Master Hatch. Give the ladies a treat, eh? They like a trifle of company.'

She opened the door and held up her lamp. The room smelled disagreeable, but not much worse than the rest of the mansion. Mrs Mitchell stood the lamp on a heavy table, which, beside a single chair, was the only furnishing, and laid the Register near it.

'Look, Polly!' she said cheerfully. 'Young man to see you!'

With grinning interest, Hatch saw the ladies. There were two of them. They were very old and secured by sensible chains to rings on either side of the grate ... somewhat after the fashion of disreputable fire-dogs.

Behind them, piled up against the wall, was their grubby bedding. Polly nodded to Mrs Mitchell, then peered inquisitively at Hatch. She was a bent old thing, whose head seemed to grow more out of one shoulder than the other.

'Evening, Polly,' said Hatch. But Polly, maybe sensing a shade of mockery in the filthy Hatch's voice, affected a dignity.

'Polly put the kettle on!' said Mrs Mitchell. Whereupon the wretched creature nodded, crawled to her feet and hobbled to the black grate, carefully holding a kettle none but she could see.

'Now – Sukey, take it off again!' said Mrs Mitchell; and, on the other side of the grate, Sukey – who was pale and fat and lost-looking – rolled over and removed Polly's kettle from the chilly hob.

'Wonderful what a little kindness will do!' murmured Mrs Mitchell proudly. 'Sane as you and me, really. Understand every word. 'Straordinary. Just a little kindness and they'll eat out of your hand. Of course, you've got to watch 'em – else they'll have your fingers off at the wrist! Now – Polly put the kettle on again – then Sukey take it off!'

Once more the piteous creatures did as they were bid – somewhat more quickly.

'Careful, Sukey! There's boiling water in it! Careful dear!'

Mrs Mitchell turned her broad face to Hatch.

'This'll show you how clever they are! It's remarkable, really. Sukey! Sukey! Oh, now you spilled it! And on poor Polly!'

At once, Polly let out a great howl of distress and clutched at her leg.

'I been scalded!' Then she began to cry and whimper and sob with a pain that was no less agonizing for being so invisibly caused. And fat Sukey looked on, consumed with meaningless guilt.

'She keeps it up for an hour, y'know. Oh yes, she's sharp enough to know what a scald feels like! All right – all right, Polly! I'll go fetch some ointment, dear!'

Again Mrs Mitchell turned to the admiring Hatch – who could not but think, with a touch of pleasure, that sooner or later the idiot in the Carmody's wagon would come down to just this.

'Won't be a moment, Master Hatch. Just have to go outside – then come back with her "ointment".' She winked broadly. 'She's sharp, that one! No fooling her unless I go outside.'

Mrs Mitchell bustled out leaving Hatch alone with the two madwomen and the Register.

Being of a more bookish than compassionate disposition, Hatch ignored the dismal creatures who squealed and blubbered in the grate and inquisitively opened the Register.

At once another world lay before him. Parsons, brandy-merchants, surgeons, spinster ladies and farmers' wives, all drawn up in neat columns of Mrs Mitchell's flowing hand; and each most lovingly paid for – by their nearest, if not their dearest. Sometimes a brother, sometimes a husband, sometimes an uncle or niece or aunt. There was Polly Usher, widow: fifty pound paid by married daughter. There was Lady Susanna Vere, likewise widow: paid for by her son. Condition, comfortable . . .

Suddenly Hatch's sharp eyes grew sharper yet. There was

Belle Carter: child. Fifty pound paid in by Mr Carter of Reigate. Condition – comfortable!

He shut the book. His brain took fire. Worlds upon worlds had just opened up.

Ever since the clownish giant had told him of the private madhouse (and fiercely urged him to go there so the idiot might be fetched), he'd suspected she was worth more than a paltry ten pound. Now he knew it. And it was better than he'd dreamed. His clever brain fairly buzzed with interesting schemes ... and Black Jack dropped out of his mind like a dead stone.

Mrs Mitchell was returning. Hatch composed himself.

'The Doctor and Parson Hall will see you now, Master Hatch,' said Mrs Mitchell, and went in to comfort her noisy ladies while her husband conducted Hatch to the doctor's parlour.

'Hatch,' said Mitchell, opening the door. 'This is Hatch.' Then he departed and the doctor, his leg up in bandages from his coaching injury, stared.

'You're not the lad! Different altogether! Did the big man send you?'

'He might have done,' said Hatch, peering round the handsome room approvingly. 'And then again, he might not.'

Parson Hall, his injured right arm hitched in a sling across his heart – as if he was mortally bound to speak only and nothing but the truth, said sternly: 'Has he got her, then?'

Hatch grinned and scratched his filthy hair.

'He might ... then again, he might not.'

'What d'you mean?' asked the doctor.

'Well,' said Hatch. 'It seems we might have made a mistake, gen'lemen. It seems I've come on a wild goose chase and troubled you for nothing.'

Here he looked honestly regretful; but Parson Hall was not entirely deceived. 'Go on,' he said evenly. 'Tell us why you think you're mistook.'

'Well, gen'lemen; though in all good faith we got an idiot

what answers to the name of Belle and has "Carter" stitched in her shawl – I just seen in your very Register that *you* got an idiot of the self-same name who's comfortable, as indeed she should be on account of the fifty pound it seems you've had for her. If you take my meaning.' He sighed and looked up to the ceiling as if to give the gentlemen every opportunity of taking his meaning and examining it at their leisure. Then he went on: 'Therefore, gen'lemen, to save awkwardness and heart-ache, I'll take meself off and go see the Carters at Reigate to see if they can shed a little light on the mystery. Maybe it's them what had two idiots?'

As Hatch delivered himself of this, he saw the doctor and the parson exchange rapid and anguished glances ... like gentlemen who have much to hide and don't know where to put it. He suspected he'd struck on a richer vein than even he had supposed.

'You're a scoundrel!' said the parson abruptly. He stared at the apologetic Hatch. His prophetical eyes were well accus-tomed to light up the dark places of the soul – and they'd just come upon a singularly inky path.

'Who? Me?' said Hatch. '*I've* done nothing. Save come here and lay me problem before you!'

Now the doctor began to bluster and grow angry: called Hatch a great many things that would have pierced a thinner skin. But Hatch saw no profit in being wounded. He stood his ground and reflected he'd nought to lose but his good name ... which, being sensible, he'd already fixed a price on.

'Forty pound,' he murmured when the doctor drew breath.
'What?'

'Forty pound, gen'lemen – and I don't go to Reigate.'

He waited – his ambitious young heart thumping. Had he gone too far? The doctor and the parson stared at one another. Hatch's hopes soared. He saw a golden future winking in the doctor's frightened eyes.

'Forty pound,' he said again. 'I ain't greedy, gen'lemen. I'm leaving you a clear ten.'

In vain for the doctor to glare and for the parson to burn him up with unearthly eyes. Hatch was smiling now.

Grimly the parson nodded to the doctor. They had been trapped by the little monster. Pray to God he knew no more than he'd said. For the conduct of their establishment was no more above reproach than anything mortal. Any loss of confidence – such as the infamous Hatch might provoke – would do them no good. Mud, once thrown, tends to stick even to the fairest garment. And Hatch, from the look of him, had brought a real broadside to discharge. They shuddered to contemplate the grand disaster if it should be known that a good half of the patients declared 'comfortable' in Mrs Mitchell's flowing hand, had been – for many a year – comfortably underground. For the which small, wooden, wormy room their nearest (if not their dearest) were even yet paying out fifty pounds a year.

'Forty pound, you said . . .?'

Hatch nodded.

'And – and you'll bring her back?'

Hatch stared. 'Oh gen'lemen! Would you make a murderer of me? Would you have me kill the goose what's just laid me a fine, forty pound egg?'

When Hatch was gone, Mitchell poked his head amiably round the parlour door.

'Ha – ha! I thought he was the Devil, you know! Such a fright, he gave me –'

'A prophetical eye, Mitchell. You've a prophetical eye,' said Parson Hall sourly.

'But of course, it were just the mud on him,' explained Mitchell seriously.

'On him and in him, Mitchell, my friend. Believe you me, Almighty God was angry when He fashioned that one out of dust. He never *breathed* into him – He roundly spat!'

9

Dr Carmody's Elixir was sweet, black and oily; and it smelled of cloves. On Fridays it was dispensed out of a large kettle, quite free of charge, down the whole length of the Argosy during the noonday halt.

This was the doctor's Bounty, and he was much esteemed for it. Everyone took it: some for rheumatism, some for bowels, some for chests. Even Mrs Arbuthnot never refused. But, though she was discreet enough to make no such open gesture of mutiny, she maintained her independence by using it as furniture polish.

The weekly task of this dispensing – together with the daily ones of minding Cassandra, minding Belle, feeding Striker and putting up the doctor's books which flew like learned thunderbolts whenever the wagon rocked over ruts and stones – fell to Tolly.

The first two Fridays Dr Carmody accompanied his new apprentice; but thereafter Tolly dispensed on his own, inquiring as he went on the ailments and afflictions of the previous week.

He was not, however, as easy at this as had been the departed Hatch – who'd had the gift of making everyone seem his especial favourite. There were some wagons where Tolly lingered; and others where he was uncomfortably brief.

Shortest of all were his visits to the wagon of the midgets – thereby giving the wrinkled little men the notion that the doctor's new apprentice was surly, proud, and above their company. It never struck them that the reason for Tolly's plain dislike of loitering was their 'dear, monstrous gen'leman' who was turned into the most domestic of giants a midget could have wished.

For now, after five Fridays, it seemed that Black Jack's wild wanderings were over at last, and he was content to be no more than a peep-show. Though his bulk and fierce aspect had occasioned uneasiness at first, all such feelings had subsided, and familiarity with his health and strength had bred a gentle contempt for it. In all save Tolly that is ... who alone knew what the huge man had been – and what he still was. He shuddered when he saw the midgets bidding the evil ruffian empty their slops, or playfully tweaking his beard. With one twist of his great hands he could have unscrewed their nut-hard little heads entire ... But he stayed peaceable and calm; so why did Tolly feel, more and more strongly, that it was a calm before some terrible storm. Had something gone awry?

'For God's sake, watch what you're at!' Tolly longed to cry out. 'He'll smash you in pieces!' But fear of bringing the disaster on, prevented his warning of it. So he hastened down the line, half expecting a storm of screams and shrieks to break out as he passed.

'You look uneasy, Master Dorking,' murmured Mrs Arbuthnot, holding out her bowl for the Elixir. She smiled thinly and jerked her ringleted head towards the *Argosy*'s prow.

'Is your master in trouble at last? His fortune in the cards is overcast, I fear. And his stars ain't too bright. Only last night, I was looking –'

'No, ma'am. The doctor's well enough.'

She pursed her lips disbelievingly.

'Then is it that poor mad soul of yours going down to hell again? Oh, I've heard her!'

'She's vastly improved,' said Tolly defensively. 'And she's had no fit in two weeks now.'

He spoke the truth. Belle's last fit (preceded as usual by her strange vision) had been fifteen days before. Though no one could have said the idiot had made great strides in understanding, she was at least on the hobble.

Tolly was justly proud of her; and so was Dr Carmody, who

put the improvement down to the Elixir – whose properties grew more various every day; but Mrs Carmody affirmed it was on account of fresh air and her own good nourishing food. 'Roses in her cheeks,' she proudly declared; though, to a cooler eye (such as Tolly's), the blooms the idiot sported in her cheeks had still a very bud-nipped air.

Mrs Arbuthnot shrugged her shoulders and vanished back into her wagon, and Tolly moved on to the end of his Friday task.

Here, Mrs Hannah, the Crown Jeweller's wife was ever pleased to see him – or anyone else, for that matter. A happy, greasy, jingly lady whose skin was always a-glitter with fine brass dust so that she had the air of being a worn but once costly Christmas present.

She took the Elixir gratefully and gave Tolly a pair of brass earrings for 'his little sweetheart up the road'. She always said this, being of a simple, romantic nature which no amount of Tolly's indignation could make a dent in.

'Take 'em, dear,' she urged. 'I wouldn't be ashamed to wear 'em myself. But Mr Hannah feels that, at our time of life, I ought to wear something more – more autumnal. More leaves than blossoms, you know . . .'

She sighed, but without malice; then jingled fatly back into her wagon where the wizened tinker was hammering away at a copper necklace of berries and leaves.

So Tolly, his kettle empty, returned towards the foremost wagon.

'Tell him he's been warned!' called Mrs Arbuthnot, sharply, as he passed by. 'Tell him Basingstoke will be his undoing. Tell him I saw a dark man again in the stars. Carmody – your hour has nearly struck.'

And Mrs Arbuthnot, to her satisfaction and surprise, saw the proud doctor's apprentice start and look dismayed.

With eyes averted he hurried on past the midgets' wagon where he chanced to see Black Jack, staring with a brooding, restless air – as if he and Fate were one.

Belle was wild about the earrings. She gave no one any peace till Mrs Carmody had fixed them in her ears. Then Cassandra was held up to see 'the pretty lady' and, after a moment's admiration, began to weep and whimper with envy and loneliness: the idiot, who had once seemed her intellectual companion, was growing up and away.

Mrs Carmody put Cassandra down and commissioned the doctor to buy her a length of yellow muslin to make a respectable gown for Belle. Her clothes were a disgrace, Mrs Carmody declared, and it was plain that no charity from the *Argosy*'s poop was going to outdo the concern of the prow.

'Now her complexion's improved, yellow will suit her very well. Don't you think so, Master Tolly?'

Tolly, being deep in a book, nodded. But that wasn't enough, and Belle began to plague him and Mrs Carmody and even the doctor with her doubts about the rival claims of yellow and blue. Which doubts were only calmed by the coming of sleep; and then they were renewed on the Saturday morning when the doctor was preparing to set forth.

They were now in the countryside before Basingstoke, and Dr Carmody, together with the other principals, was to go into Basingstoke for the necessaries of their trades.

At half after nine Striker was fetched and the doctor was ready to mount – when Tolly once more reminded him of Mrs Arbuthnot's warning of calamity at Basingstoke.

The doctor nodded and smiled sagely – as if he and Fate were too long acquainted to impose on each other. But Mrs Carmody frowned and said: 'When you've been as long on the road as we, Master Tolly, you'll know that star-happy minx promises misfortune for the doctor at every turn. But as you see, he's with us still. Heaven be praised! Mark my words, when Basingstoke's safely past (as it always is), it'll be Horsham next.'

So the doctor climbed up on the ample Striker and, looking uncomfortably like a split clothes' peg, led his little troop to

Basingstoke, with Mr Arbuthnot – who lacked his wife's ambition – fetching up the rear with a diminishing song.

Black Jack had not been of the company. Tolly was much relieved. Whatever fate Mrs Arbuthnot had seen in her cards and stars, the resurrected murderer could have had no part in it.

'Master Tolly!' said Mrs Carmody briskly. 'Be off with you and do your studying in the sunshine! And take *her* with you. How do you expect her to bloom in the shadows? Though she may think the sun shines out of your eyes, it's not the one that'll put roses in her cheeks!'

Tolly sighed, tucked the Physician's Manual he'd been studying under his arm and beckoned Belle to join him in the sun.

The morning was handsome, spreading a clean silken canopy over the fashionable trees, to whose solemnities the fields and meadows seemed to be hastening with paupers' posies of cowslips, dandelions and buttercups.

They wandered to the farthest limit of the field in which the wagons were halted. Here Tolly settled in the long grass and dispatched Belle to gather wild flowers while he read on about the varieties of madness and inflammations of the brain.

From which he learned that madness from birth is a hopeless state; but with madness coming on later, there may be grounds for cautious optimism. But very cautious, and only if there be no history of the malady in the sufferer's family.

If there is such a history, then the outlook is gloomy in the extreme ... presenting periods of well-being – sometimes quite long – which are most disastrously cut off by violence, murder or self-destruction. This is most pitiable –

Tolly looked up and stared at Belle. Which was she? She smiled and waved. Then she looked back to the wagons.

'He's watching us!' she cried.

'Who?'

'The giant.'

Tolly shivered and crouched down lower in the grass. Mrs

Arbuthnot's prophecy still haunted him; and he remembered yesterday's look on Black Jack's face . . .

'Come over here, Belle.'

She came scampering in her old sprigged muslin that, even before it had been cropped to fit her, had never been more than dowdy rubbish.

All her clothes were the wildest mixture of threadbare cut-downs and costly dresses made for a child of, maybe, five . . . then worn and worn till they'd split at their several seams.

It was as if she'd once been the darling apple of her parents' eye – then abruptly cast off when the maggot had been found.

Was that when her malady had come on then? Not from birth at all?

Grounds for cautious optimism. Tolly wondered . . . Tolly brooded. Or was she more deeply infected – through the generations – and so fated to destroy herself?

'Flowers, Tolly! Tell me what they are?'

She crouched down beside him, coughing a little with excitement, and presenting him with a posy much bruised from her eager fist.

Tolly smiled and, with a simplicity no experience could improve on, nor learning tarnish, told of the flowers as he knew them – fancying that the vacant plots in her mind could have no better seeding. Maybe they'd take root – God knew there was room enough! – and fill her head with the fragile charms of vetch, heartsease and scarlet pimpernel . . .

She'd brought other flowers, too, whose names Tolly had no notion of.

'This one, Tolly. What is this pretty one?'

She held out a white, papery blossom flying from a skinny stem like a tiny flag of surrender. Tolly shook his head. He knew it not.

'Your uncle, the sea-captain,' she urged. 'Sure he must have told you –?'

Tolly shook his head again – then looked at Belle. Her eyes

caught the sunlight and twinkled with it. He flushed in annoyance. She was laughing at him.

'Please, Tolly – your uncle, the sea-captain, *must* have told you!'

She poked the blossom into his face and tickled his nose with it. He snatched it and bade her not to be childish.

'But your uncle –'

'Leave my uncle be!'

His face grew redder yet as the justice of her mockery struck home. Perhaps he had mentioned his wise uncle more often than he'd supposed . . .

'Then you leave him, too!' cried Belle angrily, and, flinging the flowers in his face, flounced off towards the trees.

Tolly jumped up, full of remorse at losing his temper with the idiot. He pursued her – caught her by the arm so's she spun and fell. His guilt was further increased when he saw that she was in tears. He knelt.

'Belle –'

'No! No! Go off! Go back to your uncle!'

'I promise I'll not talk of him again –'

She stopped her crying so abruptly that Tolly was bewildered.

'Never again?'

'Well . . . not – not to you, Belle.'

'You'll not talk about the sea, then?'

'Not till you've seen it, Belle.'

She stared up at him, and the twinkle vaguely fluttered in the deep of her eyes. Tolly was curiously held by it. For the briefest moment he wondered if there was something more within her than madness. It was as if her wretched condition was but a garment – as eccentric as all her others – concealing a form unguessed at. He wondered if Dr Carmody's 'horny mesentery' was somewhere here, and not where the remarkable doctor supposed . . . ?

'What are you *like*, Belle?' asked Tolly, almost without meaning to.

'A poor thing,' said she, turning her head and peering into the grass. There was a note of bitterness in her voice; then she shook her head and smiled up at him.

'Tell me about the sea,' she begged; and it was plain she'd forgiven him and was releasing him from his promise not to talk of his uncle.

So Tolly sighed and told her – as he'd done this many a time – of the sea in its moods and seasons.

'Water, Belle – as far as the eye can see . . .'

'What noise does it make?'

'It sighs and whispers and slaps and sometimes roars.'

'What is it like when the wind blows?'

'Huge and terrible. It rises up in dark, shiny walls, all foamy on top. Then down it crashes and the beach stones fly.'

'What is it like when the sun shines?'

'Like a great looking-glass, Belle. Very smooth and bright and still-looking.'

'What's under the sea, Tolly?'

'Green darkness – like a great forest. Strange flowers and weeds and fish and sunken ships and treasures . . .'

Belle closed her eyes, as if to imagine it the better. Tolly observed her thin face, now placid as the sunshine sea he'd described. What green darkness lay in its depths? What queer flowers, what treasures, even?

Suddenly she opened her eyes.

'Why did you not go to sea? You love it so –'

'My uncle,' he began; then bit his lip and grinned sheepishly. 'My mother and father were killed by the sea. It seemed – unlucky . . .'

'Does it go by family, then, Tolly? The way you die, I mean?'

Tolly laughed and shook his head.

'Why no! It's not a malady like –'

He stopped, for the thought was lodged firm in his mind of maladies like Belle's. He could not tell her of what he'd read:

of maladies that haunt the generations to bring each possessor to the same sad end.

'No matter!' said Belle, sitting up and shaking her head so that Mrs Hannah's earrings jingled like infant wedding bells. 'Your uncle, the sea-captain, did very well not to let you go to sea!'

'Why?'

'Because then you'd never have found me after I'd fallen from the coach!'

Tolly's heart quickened. Here was something remarkable. For the first time she'd recalled the accident. He began to grow excited. Would she remember more? Would she remember the beginnings of her sickness? Above all, would she remember her family and –

But before he could put any of the countless questions whose answers might have strengthened his growing hopes, there came a terrible interruption.

A storm of screams and shouts broke out in the midgets' wagon!

'He's done it!' whispered Tolly, staring helpless at the wagon that shook and rocked under some horrible commotion within.

In his mind's eye he could see the enraged Black Jack pounding in the heads and chests and neat little bellies of the shrieking midgets. Blood by the bucketful – by the ocean – would henceforth be on Tolly's head ... for his had been the hand that had raised Black Jack from the dead.

Then, suddenly, like a painted egg, the wagon seemed to crack at its door and hatch the enormous ruffian in a black and furious haste.

But instead of the tide of lumpy blood that Tolly expected to gush in his wake, there hopped and leaped six midgets (four male and a pair of tiny fluttery dames) with roars and shouts of no more frightful injury than rage!

'He *didn't* do it!' whispered Tolly. 'Why?'

Black Jack had set off across the grass at what would have

been a great rate; but he was much hampered by his monkish gown (which he still wore though it stank villainously) and by something he clutched under his arm.

'Thief! Thief!' came high and shrill from tiny lungs; and Black Jack, his huge legs going like the spokes of a cartwheel, lumbered faster yet.

But the midgets were as rapid as gnats. They gained upon him, and the great ruffian, sensing his pursuers growing close, abruptly changed direction. He thundered towards Tolly.

The boy saw his face, spiked round with his ragged hair and beard like the rays of an angry black sun . . .

Tolly heard Belle cry out in fear. He put his arm about her shoulders; drew her close.

Black Jack saw the mad girl. His pace faltered. Rage and dread contended in his face; then an extraordinary flicker of jealousy. He made to turn again – but the hesitation had done for him. With shrieks of triumph, the midgets flung themselves upon him.

Tiny though they were, their sixfold fury confused the giant. He staggered, attempted to twitch them off, then to drag away. To no purpose. His legs were caught. He roared – and fell.

But even then, with four little men pinioning him by his limbs and the women by his hair, he still threshed violently – like some huge fish, before the daring fishermen silence it with an iron bar.

To Tolly, who knew full well the giant's health and

strength, it seemed certain that he'd dash their brains out. But before he could stir to drag the fierce little creatures out of death's way, most amazingly they prevailed.

The giant groaned – and gave up the fight. The midgets kicked him once or twice – then gathered up the box he'd been making off with.

'Tried to rob us,' said one of them to Tolly, rattling the box. 'A month's takings in here. Don't it make you puke, young man? A creature his size robbing tiny mites like us! He's lucky he ain't hanged for it!'

On which they returned to their wagon, having no further interest in Black Jack's life or death.

Black Jack rose to his feet. He rubbed his neck where Mister Ketch's signature had grown livid from recent strain. Then he cast such a look upon Tolly as to haunt the boy for many a dark night after. There was hatred in the look: and more. Fathoms deep, Tolly seemed to see a shifting glimmer – as if he was peering down into the giant's green soul.

Then it vanished and Black Jack, without another word or look, shambled off into the trees and was gone.

Though the loss of Black Jack should have rejoiced Tolly, somehow the manner of it cast a gloom on his spirits that infected even the excitable Belle.

But in the Wagon of Mystery there was triumph. Mrs Arbuthnot flaunted herself at Mrs Carmody.

'Perhaps now you'll pay heed to my warnings, ma'am. For let me tell you, it's not so much *him* who'll suffer, but the innocent souls he presumes to lead. A dark man at Basingstoke. I saw it; I said it; and lo, it's come to pass! So I lay to you now, step down or beware of Horsham. For Horsham will be his undoing.'

Mrs Carmody shrugged her shoulders, but there was no lowering Mrs Arbuthnot, who repeated the above (with additions) to everyone she could find – thereby somewhat overplaying her hand – so that when Dr Carmody returned from Basingstoke, everyone was so pleased to see him alive and in one piece that Mrs Arbuthnot and Black Jack were quite forgot.

It was indeed a more than ordinarily joyful homecoming; and Dr Carmody matched it. Not only had he fetched back the yellow muslin for Belle's gown but, also a green coat he'd bought off a footman for Tolly.

'Next to nothing it cost, my dear,' he said to Mrs Carmody when she reproached him with extravagance.

'What's next to nothing, Dr C? Ten pound would be next to nothing – if there's nothing in between!'

'Peace, ma'am. Now he's my apprentice, he must look well, y'know...'

And Mrs Carmody, like everyone else, looked at her husband's fine, dignified head – and helplessly nodded her own. It was indeed a countenance that had to be lived up to.

'Try it on, my boy,' said the doctor cheerfully; and Tolly exchanged his own torn and stained coat for the handsome green one.

'There! Don't it suit him? 'Tis the colour of Nature! The colour of innocence! The colour of the sea, even...'

Tolly beamed – and Belle, poking her head out of the wagon, clapped her hands with delight. Then she said, in a voice grown unusually clear and strong – as if anxious there should be no mistake or misunderstanding anywhere, 'Oh Tolly! I do love you, you know!'

Whereupon a war broke out in Tolly's heart – a war between pleasure and dismay.

'Dear God! What am I to do?' he whispered to himself. But the only answer he could presently find was in the performance of a duty long overdue.

He must, he really *must*, write to his uncle, the sea-captain. He'd know what should be done...

10

SOME three weeks after Belle had told her love to Tolly, Lord Somers of Reigate – after his father had discovered no financial or family impediment to the match – declared something after the same fashion to Miss Kate Carter one evening in Carter's mansion, between the roast capon and the cheese.

And, though the event was not entirely unexpected, its fulfilment was greeted with a joy that had more than a touch of passionate relief. Though the sun was long gone down, all the windows of the mansion made another day with candlelight; there was not a room anywhere – even among the once shuttered upper ones – that had not its little nest of suns. It was as if the Carters were wild to show the world that they'd nothing anywhere to hide; that even the natural shadows of the night had no place in a life so open as theirs.

Next morning it seemed that all of Reigate had eavesdropped – for a tide of congratulations beat upon the Carters' door. Carriages came and went and a gratifying number of cards remained to mark the neighbourhood's esteem.

But among the callers was one who had no card. A young man – little more than a lad, really, though neatly enough dressed. His manner was inquisitive, though respectful. His face was not so much thin as sharp.

'Name of Hatch,' he said. 'To see Mr Carter.'

'Not at home,' said the footman, having sized Hatch up and found him wanting in the same.

'Then I'll wait,' said Hatch, with an edging courtesy.

'P'raps I don't make myself clear,' said the footman, who, like all servants whose loyalty has long been made use of, tended to use it more as a weapon than a quality. 'The master's not at home. To you, that is. I was being genteel. If you've business, you may inform me. If you ain't, then you may go. The master,' he went on patiently, as Hatch made no sign of understanding, 'don't see tradesmen or the like. Else where would he be? So be a sensible young man and make off.'

Hatch, who could see no profit in being impudent, nodded meekly; then transferred his sharp gaze to the silver tray awash with cards.

'Happy circumstance in the offing?' he said.

The footman shrugged his shoulders.

'If I'd a card about me, I'd be pleased to leave it,' said Hatch humbly, and fished in his pockets. 'But all I've got's me Boney-Fridays; which I'd be obliged if you'd take to Mr Carter and say that Hatch is in the house.'

Whereupon he drew out Belle's tattered length of lace and laid it over the tray like a pall.

The footman stared and shuddered. His hand went to his face – for he was the ironical-looking servant who'd once been scarred by the 'poor thing'.

'How did you come by that?'

Solemnly Hatch shook his head.

'In our line of business, we don't talk over much.'

With a look of profound dismay, the footman took up the shawl and led Hatch to a small parlour to await the master of the house.

'Handsome place you got here,' said Hatch affably; but the footman answered never a word. Instead, he cast a last bitter look as he shut the door upon the neat young visitant from Hell.

It was perfectly plain that Mr Carter did not know what to expect. He had a bewildered, even frightened look on his face as he came into the room.

Hatch, rising to greet him, felt almost sorry for him; but then, with the natural strength of youth, he overcame the feeling, and smiled.

Like anyone else he had to make his way in the world and

there were worse ways of doing it than the way that had fallen to him. After all it wasn't as though he was profiting by other folks' virtue; it was rather their dark deceits that helped him on. In a way, he was a kind of scourge ... God's punishment, in fact.

'Well?' whispered Mr Carter, holding out the shawl. 'What is it? Is she – dead?'

'Why bless you, no, sir!' said Hatch, happy to be the bearer of glad tidings.

'They why...? What have you come for? Why has Dr Jones sent you? And at such a time! Good God! What a time to remind us!'

'Very unfortunate,' agreed Hatch, his ambitious young heart beating fit to burst and quite intoxicating him with excitement. 'But Dr Jones didn't exactly send me.'

'Then why –?'

'I was just passing through,' murmured Hatch, 'and thought you might like to know that ... all was well.'

'Thank you – thank you!' said Mr Carter with some relief. 'Now, please go!'

'That all was well ... *considering*,' repeated Hatch.

'Considering what?' Mr Carter's relief suffered a set-back.

'Considering that fifty pound don't go very far towards keeping a certain young lady in such circumstances as she must have been accustomed to.'

Here Hatch stared about the richly furnished parlour, and the meaning of his words sank into Mr Carter's heart and chilled it.

'But we agreed –' said Mr Carter bitterly; when Hatch shook his head.

'What you agreed with Dr Jones is between you and him, sir. This is something ... different. If you take my meaning.'

Hatch spoke gently. Mr Carter was a big man – and Hatch saw no profit in pricking him with an ill tone.

Mr Carter sat heavily in a chair – his considerable fists

clenched despairingly on his youngest daughter's shawl. He lifted his eyes as if attempting to view Hatch's soul and throw some light in that dark place.

Hatch turned away. 'Don't take it amiss, sir. I don't aim to ruin you. On my honour, I don't! All I want is to see everyone happy! I want to see a certain young person as happy as her poor condition allows. I want to see her left in peace. And that costs money. Believe me, sir – it costs a deal more than fifty pound! Oh, Dr Jones don't know the half of it!' He paused, as if he'd convinced himself and was thereby surprised.

'Then again, I want to see you and your handsome family happy. D'you think,' he went on, even waxing indignant, 'that I want all Reigate to discover you got a mad daughter kept hidden and little better off than an animal? D'you think I want to see the happy circumstance (what I understand is in the offing) blighted and come to nought? D'you think I've come all the way from Islington just to destroy you all? Oh, Mr Carter, sir – I ain't that monstrous! Believe me, sir – I've only come to reassure you! And *that* costs money!'

Hatch stopped, quite overcome by his own eloquence. He had grown. His ambition, nourished by Dr Jones's forty pound, sustained him now in a way the previous Hatch would have been amazed at.

'How much do you want?' whispered Mr Carter, his proud happiness suddenly veined with cracks to its shifting foundation.

'You're a gent!' said Hatch impulsively, and knelt at his victim's feet.

'A hundred pound is all I ask! Ain't it worth it, sir? For peace of mind!'

Helplessly Mr Carter nodded and Hatch, touched to the depths of his being murmured: 'Oh, sir! A father couldn't do more for his child! Yes, sir! You're a real father to me!'

On which Mr Carter stared down at him with something like horror. His expression remained unchanged during his brief absence from the room – only deepening in its dismay when he returned with the sum demanded ... as if he'd hoped Hatch had been no more than an evil dream.

'And the shawl, sir,' said Hatch respectfully. 'She sets great store by it, y'know. I only fetched it to show me Boney-Fridays, after all!'

Silently Mr Carter handed over the shawl which Hatch pocketed.

'She's all right, you say? She – she's alive and well?'

'Alive and kicking,' grinned Hatch amiably. 'And scratching and biting, too – from what I understand!'

Whereupon, to Hatch's pain and surprise, Mr Carter struck him in the face.

'There was no call to do that!' he cried, 'It ain't my fault she's raving mad! It's – it's God's will – that's what it is! I'm only doing what anybody else in my situation would do. You – you ought to be thankful I didn't ask for more! You ought to be thankful I'm keeping your secret –'

Of a sudden Mr Carter's fury diminished and gave way to fright. He had offended the blackmailer? Hatch rubbed his face – then smiled ruefully.

'Well, well! We both lost our tempers, sir! But now it's out of our blood and we're friends again. Nothing like a storm to clear the air, eh?'

Humbly Mr Carter agreed. There was indeed nothing like a storm to clear the air. But when that air was cleared, what was there to be seen?

Nothing but a landscape of despair. A black place where winds grew and grew till they should be reaped at last as whirlwinds.

'AND it is eleven weeks now since he's gone and still no sign of that monstrous man. Either he has been caught and hanged again – which I hope not – or he's taken up honest employment: which I doubt. But, to return to the girl. She continues to make progress towards being a rational soul. Her memory is much stronger, and her fits have disappeared entirely. Still, all depends on whether there is a history of the malady in her family. And this, I'm sure you'll agree, I *must* discover. When I have, I will come to you directly, sir –'

Thus Tolly, lying awake in his hammock under the Carmodys' wagon, composed a letter to his uncle, the sea-captain. Which letter, still unwritten, had been put off from day to day: there always being some decisive event just ahead that would make for more interesting relating.

The *Argosy* was already in Sussex, outside of Horsham (with Mrs Arbuthnot reading the stars like a daily paper, filled with calamity), and the sea was not far off.

If the letter wasn't written soon, the neglectful writer would be arriving at his uncle's door with his news still in his mouth.

The last event he'd waited on had been his first performance before the public with the Elixir, in the part that Hatch had filled so dramatically well.

But, as it had gone so unfortunately, he'd done what he could to strike the episode from his mind. None the less, it haunted him . . .

There had been a prosperous crowd all right; and the doctor had been in fine voice. He'd held out the bottle and Tolly had skilfully snatched it and scuttled off among the tumbled skirts and legs. So far, so good. But further worse: even disastrous. He'd popped up beside a stout, motherly soul who was so used to grabbing noxious bottles out of the thieving hands of her brood, that she never thought twice about doing the same for Tolly. Before he could so much as sip the Elixir, she'd snatched it away with, 'What does a respectable, cheerful boy like you want with that nasty rubbish?' Then she'd pressed a sixpence into his startled hand and said: 'Go buy some nourishing ale!'

From which humiliation, though it was now nearly a month old, he'd not yet recovered. He felt that the Carmodys were disappointed in him and regarded him as a poor exchange for the more brilliant Hatch.

Not that Dr Carmody's outward manner had changed. Wisdom and benevolence shone in his face as ever, and spread confidence wherever he was . . . even in his own wagon.

Mrs Carmody herself – though she'd known the doctor this many a long year – still nourished the belief that one day he'd burst out and whatever was behind that powerful countenance would amaze the world and justify her solid faith. Often she'd look at him and shake her head as if to say, 'There *must* be something more!'

Everyone expected great things of the doctor. (Even Mrs Arbuthnot conceded that the calamity for which he was heading would be a sizeable affair.) But what these great things were, none could say. Not even the doctor himself had a very clear idea of how, when and where he was going to burst out. However, everyone's faith in him continued to justify his own, thus his God-given countenance radiated a hope that eternally fed on what it gave. So Tolly, in spite of all misfortune, continued to draw comfort from it, and even inspiration . . .

He went on with his proposed letter, now murmuring it aloud as notion tumbled on notion in the softly creaking darkness of his hammock; from where he sought to impress his upright uncle that his strange apprenticeship was bearing fruit and that he had not abandoned drapery for any idle frivolity.

'As I was saying, sir – about the girl . . . The dusty look she once had is gone. One might suppose the fresh air has blown it away and given her a sort of bloom that – that is almost handsome. The yellow gown that Mrs Carmody made for her, sets her off tolerably . . . and now ones sees that she is beginning to fill out and become quite womanly. If only one might be sure that –'

'That what, Tolly?'

Belle's voice, coming from above, broke distractedly in. The gap in the wagon's boards, enlarged by the devious Hatch, had never quite been made good. Consequently it furnished a murmuring passage for Belle and Tolly through which they wished each other their private good nights.

Tolly wondered how much Belle had overheard. He pictured her, lying or crouching above him, her cloudy hair engulfing her small, wild face and kissing the boards. He reached up to see if a strand was fallen through. The hammock swung and grunted.

'Tolly! I know you're awake. I can hear you –'

'Listeners at door and floors hear no good of themselves,' muttered Tolly peevishly.

'You said I looked pretty in my yellow dress.'

'Tolerable, Belle. That's all I said.'

'And womanly,' went on Belle, a satisfied note in her voice. In the absolute darkness, Tolly reddened.

'I'm pleased you've noticed,' said Belle proudly. 'Mrs Carmody says she'll have to let out my dress to accommodate me. She says she's never known a bosom swell so vigorously handsome in the summer sun. She says it's her cooking –'

'It's only in the course of nature,' muttered Tolly awkwardly.

'Don't you like it, then?'

'Yes, yes. Of course. Very elegant. Go to sleep, Belle.'

Here, there was a longish pause in which the chirpings and twitterings of the summer's night contended with the thumping of Tolly's heart.

'You're not asleep.'

Silence. Tolly declined to answer.

110

'I can see you –'

A feeling of alarm seized the boy. He stared up and fancied he could see the glimmer of an alien eye.

His uneasiness grew. Belle's eyes disturbed him. Though the old blandness had passed from her features and freed them for rapid animation, her eyes were still patched with little blanknesses ... as if her malady was but withdrawn and had left behind these misty flags of a further intent.

What was happening in her pretty head? What secret creatures were at work, nibbling at the substance of her mind till it should collapse in wispy ruin...?

Horror at his thoughts drove Tolly to hide his head in his blanket – away from whatever watching there might have been.

'Tolly – why won't you answer?'

'I – I'm sleepy ...'

'I love you –'

'Go to sleep, Belle –'

'I can't sleep, Tolly. Not till you tell me that you love me ...'

Desperately Tolly looked into his heart to see how best he might answer.

In vain to turn to thoughts of his uncle, the sea-captain. No help there. His uncle was an iron bachelor, quite proof against arrows in the heart: no female in his neat life or in his neat house save his housekeeper, a pebbly lady somewhat resembling a ship's figurehead, being more the hard, glazed notion of a woman than the warm, soft fact ...

The image of Belle, so close above him, grew in his mind to enormous dimensions, threatening to engulf him with her half-mad 'Do you love me?'

'Tolly –'

'Yes, Belle ...'

She laughed softly.

'What are you laughing at?'

'You said you loved me. I asked you, and you answered,

"Yes, Belle." Now it's settled. We'll be together always. When will you marry me, Tolly?'

Though the night was warm, Tolly felt chilled to the bone by the scope of the disaster into which he'd fallen. Now it was settled. Always.

Belle was still laughing, very gently and with an air of amorous mockery.

'When will it be, dear Tolly? This year . . . next year?'

'Some time, Belle –'

Her laughter ceased on the instant.

'Or – never?' she muttered. 'Why did you take me with you out of the wood? Wouldn't it have been a mercy if I'd done myself a mischief? Wouldn't I be better off dead?'

Her voice was grown so low and unsteady, that Tolly could scarce make out her unhappy words.

'When I've finished my apprenticeship, Belle,' he whispered quickly – and was surprised by how cheerful his words sounded against the misery that begot them. 'When I've enough money to look after you, Belle. When we've found a place to live in . . . a house, or a cottage, maybe. Or even a ship . . . when we've found a fine ship, Belle, and our course is set. When the wind blows fair and the sea's as calm as a looking-glass . . . when – when the stars fall down from the sky . . . when –'

He stopped. Above him was now the breathing silence of a wagonload of sleep. He prayed that he might join in; and presently began to drift and drift . . .

'Tolly – Tolly . . . are you there? Tolly – Tolly –'

Like an undertow, the voice dragged him back. It was low and whispery. Was it Belle? Or even Dr Carmody? All whispers are alike – as if to mark that, in secret, all souls are alike . . .

It was very close, and accompanied by unequal breathing. It was not from above, but from beside.

Tolly peered over the edge of the hammock. Staring at him,

huge and tragic, was the face of Black Jack! He had come back.

Lanterns! Lanterns! Lanterns! Rocking and swinging out of the backs of wagons making them yawn like painted mouths.

Now they bobbed about, magically producing faces out of the night. Anxious, inquisitive faces ... There was Mrs Arbuthnot, neatly shawled, never took by surprise – to the aggravation of other ladies whose hair was in as many twisted papers as a lawyer's account.

She peered and stared and muttered; but was not triumphant on her reading of the stars. For, though a dark man was come at Horsham, he was not what she'd fearfully hoped.

He lay in the grass, breathing harshly and moaning the while. He was very gaunt-looking and tangled and torn. If any hour had been struck, it looked to be Black Jack's, and the proud doctor had escaped again.

But quiet, now! Quiet! His lips were moving. He was trying to speak. Immense effort. Dried blood clung about his mouth ...

What was he saying? The boy – the doctor's apprentice – bent close.

'Food and drink!' said Tolly urgently.

'For ... pity's sake –' whispered Black Jack. 'Afore – I'm – gone ...'

Mr Arbuthnot, mysterious maker of sausages, fetched a dish of his wares. Lantern lit, they looked alive. And brandy. Brandy out of a nondescript bottle, handed eagerly to Tolly by the nondescript wagoner who mumbled something, then retired into his customary shadows. Jed, or Jem his name was. No one ever really heard him clear.

Tolly raised Black Jack's ravaged head, which was heavy on his neck – like a spent thunderbolt – and gave him a drink.

He coughed and seemed to choke, then signed for Tolly to

113

lower his head again, closing his eyes when this was done. For a moment it was thought he'd died; then his eyes opened and a strengthening light was seen in them. Once more he fought to speak: laid out every scrap of his strength as if his utterance was vastly important. But by dint of careful listening, it proved to be no more than, 'Thank ... you ...'

Then, seeing he'd made himself understood, he closed his eyes once more and seemed to have gone off into a deep sleep.

Now Dr Carmody, Mr Arbuthnot, Mr Hannah, Jed (or Jem) and Tolly lifted him up off the dampish ground and carried him into the nondescript wagon, having understood the mumbling of its owner as being an offer of Christian charity. Here he was to continue his sleep.

Tolly would not leave him, and, for the rest of the night sat by his head, remembering and remembering the last time he'd sat by Black Jack's quiet body: in Mrs Gorgandy's grim parlour, one evening in April, long ago.

As became his size, Black Jack slept for a great while; but Tolly never left him, fearing that, should he awake alone, he'd fly into a panic and thereby do some unnecessary mischief.

It was past midday when he opened his eyes, and Tolly was much relieved to see the improvement had been sustained.

'It's me little saint,' mumbled Black Jack, grinning faintly and revealing teeth distressingly broken and ground down by his poor harsh diet of the weeks that had gone. Which diet, in its latter stages, had torn his lips when he'd lacked strength to break off the spikes and spines of such berries and roots as he'd thrust into his mouth.

Black Jack had been living wild. But none too well, it seemed; and now, when his endurance was come to its end, he would see Tolly once more.

'I ... I thought,' muttered Tolly, 'that you'd have managed, Black Jack.'

114

Black Jack stared at him – and a flicker of his old scorn seemed to come back.

Tolly said: 'Surely you could have – have used your health and strength? I mean – just once or twice – couldn't you have – have stole something to keep you going? Weren't there no inns or coaches, Black Jack?'

(Dear God above! What would his uncle, the sea-captain, have said to such advice?)

Black Jack's eyes were frightened and bitter.

'Aye, there were inns and coaches, Tolly.'

'Then why –?'

Black Jack raised his hand and pointed to his neck – still invoiced by the law of the land.

'There was ... pain. Pain such as you don't know of, Tolly. Deep, 'orrible, sharp and strangling ... I been 'anged 'alf a 'undred times, Tolly. It was as if all the dead and rotted Mister Ketches were risen up to claim me for 'aving defaulted. And each with his length of rope, Tolly. For whenever ...'

And then, with bleak despair, he told of his strange condition. Whenever he'd made to attack and rob – even though it had been but for the sake of his health and strength – there'd been so hideous and implacable a pain in his neck (about the site of Mr Ketch's operations), that he'd been unable to move.

Had Tolly never heard him screaming with it? For it seemed to him, Black Jack, that all the world must have heard him in his wilderness.

But Tolly hadn't heard. Much ashamed, he shook his head.

He was startled to feel Black Jack gripping his hand, villainously tight. He'd been quite unaware that all this while the huge man's hand had been resting round his own.

Black Jack peered up at him. There was no contempt now.

'I'm finished, Tolly. I'm disabled for me trade. What's there left for me in the world? What's the use of me? What am I, Tolly, but a poor great thing what should 'ave been 'anged?'

And then, like Belle before him, he laid his burden on Tolly's unlucky, gentle heart.

'Why did you save me, Tolly? For God's sake, why didn't you leave me to choke in me coffin where I might 'ave come to peace at last?'

12

HOPING to pass unremarked in the gaudy caravan from which there seemed no escape (for he had a passion for being inconspicuous), Jed had painted scenes of Oriental splendour and junketing all over his nondescript wagon. Unluckily it had rained before the paint had properly dried, so there still showed through, in the Eastern sky, I BUY AND SELL ANYTHING — like a warning from some divine Banker to the heedless spendthrifts below.

But inside the wagon there was quite a homely, even romantic air ... what with a pair of broken hobby-horses, a family of wounded dolls and several curious wooden objects that had never been sold on account of no one ever knowing what they were for. Also, round the walls was hung a collection of playbills from Greenwich, Bristol and Richmond in Yorkshire. Jed, in his days of freedom, had been a great traveller and lover of the Stage.

It was in these surroundings that Black Jack slowly recovered his health and strength. Dr Carmody visited him regularly, but never could persuade him to take the Elixir. Not even Tolly could do that. Black Jack's nourishment came instead from Mrs Carmody's good cooking, Jed's brandy, and, once in a while, Mr Arbuthnot's sausages — which he brought secretly and hoped that the stars in their courses and the cards in their suits would have more important matters than this to confide to his unknowing wife.

But, having far to go, Black Jack's nourishing took time to show effect. It was not till the beginning of September that there came out of Jed's wagon a reasonable likeness of the mighty ruffian who'd once been hanged.

Even then he never stayed out long. It was as if his sojourn in the wilderness had left him with a strong dislike of the open sky — be it never so kind and sunny.

Or perhaps it was the presence of the midgets he'd once tried to rob that put him off. They alone never spoke to him or seemed to notice him. Little as they were, they were inclined to be hard and unforgiving ... as if, by being compressed into a small space, their natures had lost softness with size.

Or maybe he was made uneasy by the unending trickle of Horsham townsfolk who still came to wander, stare and spend among the enticing wagons. Or was it only the homeliness of Jed's wagon that drew him back into it ... to listen to more of Jed's mumbled tales of the wonderful plays behind the playbills? As Jed's conversation always seemed to come out as shy and awkward grunts, it was doubtful if Black Jack got much benefit from it.

Tolly visited him twice a day; but more of silence passed between them than comfortable talk. The huge man would sit and stare, with a deep, defeated air at ... at nothing in particular.

Vainly Tolly tried to interest him in something outside of himself: even in Belle.

'She's improved so much, Black Jack – you'd not know her now ...'

Black Jack nodded and nodded and peered round at the playbills.

'Othello,' he said vaguely. 'A tale about a handkerchief ... It haunts, me, Tolly –'

Tolly frowned at the giant's abstraction and entire failure to hear what he'd said.

'Her eyes shine and her mind's almost clear, Black Jack,' Tolly went on firmly – still hoping to fetch the sunken giant up into the sun. 'If only she can remember her name and where she's from, then – then all would be well! For sure to God there's no madness in her family!'

'A handkerchief with strawberries on it,' muttered Black Jack forlornly. 'And then a damned strangling. Oh Lord! Was our necks made for nothing else?'

But on the morning of the move from Horsham, his spirits seemed to improve a little. He was even seen to smile when Mrs Arbuthnot loudly predicted that the Carmodys' pride would have a fall ... either at Crawley (the next halt), or shortly after.

Once more, the Arbuthnots had been outflanked, outpaced and very nearly rammed by the subtle Mrs Carmody who'd beat them to the road. For the rest of that morning, which was a Friday, Mrs Arbuthnot sat beside her husband, her dark eyes flashing and her bosom heaving with thwarted ambition. As always, in front of them lumbered another wagon ... never the winding, mysterious road, symbol of the future which she regarded as her especial interest and right.

At the noonday halt Tolly and Belle came down the line with the great kettle of Dr Carmody's Elixir.

'I wouldn't give it to a dog!' said Mrs Arbuthnot coldly; and emptied her panful into the road at Tolly's feet.

Her voice carried clear to the *Argosy*'s prow. There was a moment's silence, then Mrs Carmody was heard to declare contemptuously that there was more of Mystery and Prediction in Cassandra's arse than in all the Arbuthnots' shabby wagon put together.

Tolly grinned – then hurriedly drew Belle off. He hoped that her smile on Mrs Carmody's epigram had been missed by the suddenly witch-like Mrs Arbuthnot.

'Morn, Toll!' greeted Jed, jug in hand and beam on face. 'Come'n in?'

Tolly looked at Jed. The nondescript wagoner laid his finger to the side of his nose and nodded. Tolly's heart beat quick. He glanced sideways at Belle. Very presentable. This was to be her first visit. On previous Fridays, Jed had shaken his head. But now he'd nodded. So at last the giant had been persuaded out of his horror of madness; or, rather, he'd yielded to Tolly's urgings that the terrible seeds in Belle's mind had been blown away for ever.

'This is her, Black Jack,' said Tolly nervously: and Belle, anxious in her yellow gown, came out from behind Tolly and approached the sombre giant.

She'd brought him a bunch of flowers which she now offered – much as if she expected him to eat them. Whereupon Jed, who'd effaced himself in the shadows like one of his own unsaleable objects, hastened forward and took the posy out of Belle's trembling hand – where it might well have stayed for ever. Then, with an air of bemused tenderness, he thrust it into the jug of Elixir he was still holding and shuffled back into the shadows, where he lurked, with the flowers up to his nose, so that his hair rising above them resembled a species of strange foliage.

Black Jack looked long at Tolly, then at Belle. She smiled uneasily, and reached for Tolly's hand. But Black Jack was hard put to it for an answering smile.

Very bleak and desolate was his vast face – even a tufted wilderness unto itself – as he saw the frail, unsettled girl who clutched on to Tolly's hand.

'Cured, you say ... a miracle, you say ... wonderful – wonderful,' he muttered; while his sunk eyes expressed no such thing.

Belle glanced at him with a puzzled frown; and Black Jack returned it with interest. Hopefully Tolly waited on the monstrous ruffian's better approval.

'Ten pound,' said Black Jack inexplicably. 'We should have settled for less. I wish –'

But Black Jack's wish – whether for joy or disaster – was not to be known.

The wagon's back had burst open. Dark in the glaring sunlight stood a shawled figure. It was Mrs Arbuthnot.

'Sneer and laugh to your hearts' content!' she shouted, pointing violently at Tolly and Belle. 'You will be brought down along with your proud master!'

'But, ma'am –' began Tolly.

'Don't ma'am me! I saw you grin – you and that daft bitch

too! If not at Crawley, then at Reigate, my friends! At Reigate you'll be crushed! I tell you – there's no escape! It's in the stars!'

So incensed was Mrs Arbuthnot, that she scarce noticed her husband was come to draw her back to their own wagon. She continued to shout:

'Reigate! That'll crush you! Reigate – Reigate!' till Mr Arbuthnot gave a stronger tug and the enraged soothsayer shrieked and vanished.

The canvas flap fell back and cut off the sunlight as with a knife. The powerful, venomous words of Mrs Arbuthnot seemed to remain in the dim wagon – enjoying a silence. From outside could be heard – even yet – her voice crying faintly, 'Reigate ... Reigate ...' like the jealous witch's christening curse.

'Reigate ... Reigate ...'

Now it was Belle. Tolly stared at her. Jed seemed to lean forward out of his thicker shadows. There was a thump and a splash as he dropped the jug of Elixir. But no one minded him. Black Jack creaked on his couch. His eyes vanished into dark pools overhung by his rocky brows. He, too, was watching Belle.

Her eyes were wide – unnaturally so. Her face was pale. She was shaking. Yet she continued to stare with the utmost fixity at a patch of air midway between the wagon's walls – as if it was suddenly populous with an air-hung drama stepped out of the crumpled playbills.

'What is it? What have you seen?'

Black Jack's voice was low and harsh – almost fearful. Tolly grew cold. He'd a terrible fear it was Belle's vision returned. He made to hold her. But, gently, she eased him away, though not letting go of his hand.

Her expression softened. Her colour returned – even with interest. She was blushing.

'My name is Belle Carter,' she said. 'And my home is in Reigate'

121

Then she looked round somewhat shyly at the strange company in the wagon – as if for some sort of approval that her malady was at last ended and that she was whole and well again.

'Belle –' breathed Tolly with awe.

'Carter,' said she, her confidence increasing when she saw the look of stupefied joy on her dear Tolly's face. 'Of Reigate, you know.'

'Belle!' said Tolly again – as if all speech, thought, passion and hope were contained in that single word.

He did not trust in his own powers to say more. Indeed, all his interior strength at that moment was employed in holding back a real waterfall of happy tears and a strong desire to jump and dance and sing and generally burst out of the wagon's roof in a manner that would have quite appalled his stately uncle.

Then Belle, with an air of great determination, poked her face in front of Tolly's and kissed him. And Tolly, not wanting to keep in debt, kissed her back . . . and found her lips warmer and softer than ever he'd dreamed possible.

'Well done!' mumbled Jed, managing a degree of clearness he'd never before achieved; and he beamed with pride that so signal a wonder should have been vouchsafed to his own nondescript wagon.

Now Tolly turned to Black Jack, who had not spoken. The huge murderer that Tolly had once resurrected, stared back at him. And still he did not speak. Instead, out of his formidable eyes ran tears as sharp as vinegar. His saviour, his eternal creditor, was lost to him for ever . . . even to a creature he could have broken with his little finger.

'Aye . . . well done . . .'

She remembered – she remembered! Dr Carmody, put out that the miracle had taken place out of his presence (and even out of his wagon), was sensible enough to be delighted; and generously took full responsibility and credit for the wonder.

'I've done it! I've done it!' he cried, warmly shaking Tolly by the hand; and with a face like his, who could doubt it?

Not Tolly, whose brightest dream had been fulfilled and who was too excited to care exactly how.

Belle remembered. The last curtain in her mind, 'the horny mesentery' as Dr Carmody would have it, had been drawn aside: and there waited her unharmed childhood.

She remembered her home – a spacious house with countless rooms, grandly proportioned to the eyes of a child ... filled with light and candles and the coming and going of courteous faces ...

'Servants,' murmured Dr Carmody shrewdly.

'Belle –' whispered Tolly.

She remembered a mother, a father and a sister, too. Misty beings of exceptional beauty (she laughed) whose hands were soft and whose clothes rustled silkenly ...

'Well-to-do,' divined Dr Carmody.

'Belle!' sighed Tolly ... with perhaps a note of sadness in his voice that her grandness was taking her out of his more humble star.

Then she remembered a strange and eerie day in which she seemed to be both dreaming and yet awake. A queer day in which time shifted in a changed direction, moving sideways so that events seemed side by side and no longer in sequence. Morning, night and morning were all wild bedfellows under the same tempestuous counterpane ... while huge, grave faces came and peered, then flew up and away, then back and back again as if they'd never gone ...

'The onset of her fever,' whispered Dr Carmody.

Then, in an evil twinkling, her whole house was swallowed up into nothingness – leaving only a small dark room, into which –

Here she frowned and shook her head. She could remember no more.

'A mercy,' breathed Mrs Carmody. 'The poor thing.'

Belle looked at her quickly – then smiled and shrugged her

shoulders. All was gone; even her strange vision. With all his heart, Tolly prayed that it might never return; for now it seemed the very insignia of her madness...

This wonderful day was the second Friday in September, at Crawley. Tolly made a solemn promise to himself that he would write to his uncle, the sea-captain, and tell him everything. In three weeks time. For in three weeks, the painted *Argosy* would be coming into 'harbour' at Reigate.

His joy was intense. It spread itself everywhere, flowing like twinkling waters into every nook and cranny and solemn cave of the *Argosy*'s hearts. People were inclined to smile for no known reason ... save that they'd caught it off Tolly – or maybe off Belle.

It was a real plague of cheerfulness. But, as in all plagues, there were some who escaped infection. Mrs Arbuthnot survived without a trace of a smile.

Indeed, she regarded the whole affair as an affront to herself and her unreliable informers, the cards and stars.

Nonetheless, she was too loyal to abandon faith openly in them, so she went about in a state of unquenchable gloom, muttering forlornly, 'Reigate. Reigate will see them all crushed.'

*

'– If any man can show just cause why they may not be lawfully joined together, let him now speak or else hereafter for ever hold his peace.'

Mr Carter held in his breath till his strained face seemed to take dye from his blood-coloured coat.

But none spoke forth; no sharp-eyed devil appeared among the brilliant wedding guests in Reigate church.

'Man and wife,' pronounced the vicar; and it was done. Kate Carter was Lady Somers – once and for all.

Dazed with relief, Mr Carter began to breathe again, and the sweat ran down from under his wig, mingling in his eyes where it imitated tears.

Hatch had missed his chance. A somewhat ghastly smile stretched itself upon Mr Carter's lips ... which, together with the moisture now running down his cheeks, was taken as a sign of joy on his daughter's happiness, and sadness on losing her.

But the passion that provoked them was quite otherwise. Since Hatch's visit, he'd lived in the hellish expectation of the blackmailer's return. Every day, every hour had become his enemy till it was past; for each might have brought with it, Hatch to his door, Hatch at his window, Hatch in the church porch to pluck at him, or Hatch in the holy church itself ...

'My dear sir! Bear up! You must make up your mind that you've not lost a daughter, but gained a son!' cried the vicar, cheerfully clinking glasses with him: and Mr Carter realized that somehow – for he'd no clear notion of even leaving the church – they were all returned to the mansion and the hubbub of rejoicing was everywhere.

'You must make up your mind, sir!'

Mr Carter – his smile no less ghastly – nodded. He had made up his mind.

Now a great and nervous haste informed all his actions. He was here, there and everywhere. Toasts he proposed with tongue-twisting rapidity ...

'To the cappy hupple – ha-ha! – happy couple!'

Everyone laughed good-naturedly at the excited father, who never stopped smiling till the new Lady Somers and her husband were safely gone off in their carriage, and Mrs Carter in a second carriage (for she was to accompany them to France), and all the merry, red-faced wedding guests in their carriages till at last the mansion was emptied of all but the father and his servants.

Then Mr Carter stopped smiling. He took down a pistol, primed it with steady hands – then laid it on the writing table in the small parlour. When Hatch should call again, Mr Carter had resolved to destroy him.

Quite suddenly, a better thought struck him. He took out a

sheet of writing paper and a pen. The look on his face was grown lighter. His smile returned, but it had lost its ghastliness and become almost gentle. He pushed the pistol to one side and began to write.

Sir: You have neglected your duty and betrayed my trust. I have been the victim of blackmail. But I will not continue so. I would rather my tragedy be shouted from the house-tops than I would spend another day in fear of so vile a creature as Hatch. Therefore, I charge you to fetch back my unfortunate child, Belle Carter, directly. I want my daughter home again. Without delay, sir. Bring her.

He sealed and franked the letter and addressed it to Dr Jones at Islington.

A great load was fallen from his mind. With Kate married, what further need for concealment? Let the world say what it would. If the blackmailer returned, he'd be met with contempt; there was no need for murder.

The letter was dispatched on September eighteenth and Mr Carter congratulated himself on the nearness of his escape. A tragedy had been averted.

But all the while, unregarded, the primed pistol remained on the writing table in the little parlour . . .

13

HATCH - respectable, prosperous and, it must be admitted, extravagant Hatch – was hurt and disappointed by his reception at Dr Jones's establishment in Islington. The doctor greeted him with a fury more suited to an inmate than to the proprietor. And Parson Hall was scarcely better controlled. He had called at a bad time. Mr Carter's letter had arrived.

'You treacherous little devil!' shouted the doctor, laying hold on the sleeve of Hatch's new coat and dragging him into the hallway.

'S-such treatment, sir – what's wrong?' cried Hatch, fearful for his safety. Parson Hall had grimly shut the front door and was glaring at him with unearthly rage.

'What's wrong?' nearly screamed the doctor. 'You've been to Reigate, that's what's wrong! You've stuck your vicious little fingers in Carter's pocket; that's what's wrong! And you mistook your man – that's what's wrong!'

'And you broke your word to us; that's what's wrong,' added the sombre parson.

'Now he wants his idiot back,' groaned the doctor, releasing Hatch who had the grace to tremble and turn white. 'And we ain't got her.'

'Where is she, Hatch?' demanded Parson Hall, pointing a prophetic finger at the blackmailer. 'Your only chance is to fetch her to us. Directly!'

Hatch stared from one to the other of the two gentlemen. Of a sudden, he saw they were more frightened than he. He saw ruin in their eyes; which sight gave him back some confidence. Hatch had a wonderfully quick wit. In other circumstances, he might have made a great statesman or an attorney . . .

But the present circumstances pressed too close for broad conjecture. Hatch said: 'I – I'm not sure where she is. Not sure exactly, that is.'

'How long to find her, Hatch?'

'A – a few days.'

Parson Hall looked to Dr Jones. They had no choice but to wait. If only Mr Carter could be persuaded to do likewise.

'A week, then,' muttered Dr Jones. 'We'll give you a week.'

'What if I can't find her?' asked Hatch – who liked to know where he stood, now that he was reasonably certain he'd be left in a condition to stand at all.

Dr Jones glared at him and was about to utter some terrible threat, when the parson, with his deeper knowledge of such souls as Hatch's, said smoothly: 'Let's not think about it that way, my son. Let's put it this way. Fetch her back and your future's assured. Say, a hundred pound on delivery and – and fifty pound a year?'

Hatch beamed. 'Done, gen'lemen. It's a bargain.' He paused. Shifted from foot to foot.

'Well?' said Dr Jones irritably. 'What are you waiting for?'

'Something on account; to show your Boney-Fridays,' said Hatch politely. 'Say – fifty pound?'

'Ten,' said Parson Hall.

'Thirty-five?' said Hatch.

'Twenty,' said Parson Hall.

'Twenty-five,' said Hatch, 'and I'm off like an arrer.'

Dr Jones paid him, and Hatch departed with quite satisfactory haste.

When the door was shut on him, the two desperate gentlemen in the hallway of their private madhouse – with cries and shouts and strange laughter proceeding faintly from upstairs rooms – stared at one another.

'Don't lose a moment, Jones!' muttered Parson Hall. 'Drive to Reigate at once!'

The doctor looked at his adviser and friend.

'And who will drive me?' he asked bitterly. The parson frowned. From the gentlemen's side, the sounds of shouts and angry shrieks and banging of chains grew louder. It was as if

128

an outing of ghosts was returned to find grave doors locked against them.

'Damn Mitchell,' said Parson Hall, with an air of pronouncing sentence.

Mr Carter's letter was not the only disaster they'd suffered. Mitchell the Under-Keeper and coachman had recently been spirited away. Which is to say, he'd shipped a great quantity of spirits at the Angel Inn and in the doomful drunkenness that had followed, he'd taken the King's shilling off a recruiting sergeant. However, as he'd been hauled off to glory and Lord Delawar's regiment on the other side of Town, he'd shouted towards the madhouse that none was to miss him as the final whirlwind was on its way and would quickly sweep them together again. But as this awesome event had been delayed, the madhouse was still without a coachman.

Parson Hall said abruptly: 'I'll fetch someone from the Angel. It's worth a pair of guineas.'

'Public coach would be cheaper,' said the doctor – who was impulsive in all things save expense.

'But slower, Jones. You must forestall that little thief.'

'But –' said the doctor; and the parson shook his head. In Hatch, they were dealing with someone quite supernaturally deceitful and treacherous. Parson Hall had no doubt he was off, not to fetch Belle, but to bleed Mr Carter for the last time.

'Then –' said the doctor; and the parson nodded. Hatch hadn't trusted them. Once the idiot had been delivered he suspected he might whistle for his money.

'But why –?' began the doctor; and the parson smiled. The twenty-five pound? A trifle. But if they'd given him nothing, then he'd have known they hadn't believed him. Oh, the parson knew his man. With twenty-five pound in his pocket, Hatch would loiter in the belief he really had the promised week.

'So you must go to Reigate at once, my friend. No delay. There's a chance you may talk Carter out of his notion.

There's a chance you may still salvage something. Believe me, my friend, that twenty-five pound may well be our salvation ... so to speak.'

But Parson Hall had overestimated Hatch, who was but sixteen and not so measured in his thinking ... He'd not the parson's skill in putting himself into his adversary's shoes, then back into his own and acting accordingly. Hatch, when he stepped into another man's shoes, did so with the object of stealing them.

Thus, when he left the madhouse, he ran as fast as his short, strong legs would carry him in the direction of Southwark from where a coach was to depart for Reigate at half after one.

He never troubled to ask himself why he'd got the twenty-five pound off the doctor. Instinct told him there was no more to come from Islington. Instinct likewise told him that, unless he got to Mr Carter without delay, there'd be no more to come from Reigate, either.

By the time Parson Hall had finished explaining to Dr Jones how Hatch's cunning mind would be working, Hatch was already in Rag Street and well on his way to London Bridge.

He was in Cheapside when the black madhouse carriage was brought out with its new coachman; and when Parson Hall was laying his strong, somewhat hairy hand reassuringly on his impulsive friend's sleeve, Hatch was upon London Bridge itself. He caught the Reigate coach with fifteen minutes to spare. Now the madhouse carriage moved away. Within, sat Dr Jones – a stoutish, sober-suited gentleman, quite alone to the passing eye. But he was not alone. Facing him, in the empty, buttoned seat, sat Ruin. A grisly individual who whispered every rattling yard of the way of Inquiries and Writs and Prosecutions for fraud, and Bailiffs and doctors in Gaol with no hope of release –

'Dr Jones, sir! Dr Jones!'

A voice broke in on his dismal thoughts. A familiar voice,

shouting as the carriage passed. The doctor stuck his head out of the window.

'Dr Jones! It's me!'

A soldier, in red coat and blue breeches – a splendid oaf – was waving. It was Mitchell. With him were four or five brown suited Biblical Brethren of the sourest, most fanatical variety. Mitchell had a wild, proud look in his eye. He shouted again and the doctor fancied he heard: 'Off to preach! Mill Yard Chapel! It's coming! End of the world! Tell the Parson and –'

His voice was lost in the rattle of carriage wheels and the doctor was left with the vanishing sight of the lunatic guardsman with his grim dark apostles, hastening him off like a scarlet firebrand in their midst . . .

The doctor drew in his head. He was quite shaken by the coincidence of Mitchell's formidable prophecy breaking in on his journey.

'Hurry, man! Hurry! It's a matter of life and death!'

The coachman, infected by the doctor's urgency, made good speed. They rocked and rattled through the countryside as wildly as if Mitchell himself had been at the reins.

Indeed, had they but left Islington a shade earlier, they'd have been in Reigate ahead of the public coach. Even so, the steaming horses had scarcely been unharnessed when they passed the Inn Yard.

But the passengers were already gone: some into the inn; some into the town; and one, on short, strong legs, to the mansion of Mr Carter.

It was some minutes after six o'clock and the light was failing. A close, somewhat oppressive evening. Several of the mansion's windows were open.

Hatch grinned. If the weather itself seemed to be in his favour, how could he fail? He hurried along the edge of the drive. He kept well in the shadows.

In all things now he obeyed his instincts – which shrewd advisers had persuaded him he wouldn't be welcome at the front door. He crept round the house, peering in window after window till at last he came to the small parlour where he'd met with such signal success before.

His grin widened. Silently he thanked the appropriate party for having blessed him with such sound instincts.

Within, in a high-backed chair, eyes closed and an unsuspecting smile on his face, sat Hatch's dear victim: Mr Carter himself. One of his hands lay in his lap; the other rested on the small writing table that had been drawn up beside him. The window was open ... to admit such air as there was. It also admitted Hatch ...

'Thank God we're here!' cried Dr Jones, as his carriage came to a halt in the Carters' drive. Hastily, he climbed out and hurried to the front door. He raised the knocker and banged once, twice. And then the house forestalled him.

A third bang came of its own accord. A loud and terrible bang that rattled the windows and shook the doctor's heart!

14

TOLLY and Belle – Belle and Tolly ... Whichever way round, they were not to be separated. Even when the knife of sleep parted them, they inhabited each other's dreams...

Theirs was a curious love – unlike any other that either of them had ever heard of. Though Belle had been the first to declare it, Tolly believed its origins to have been much earlier. It was possible to point to symptoms of it, Tolly explained, even as long ago as in the April wood when first they'd met.

'Oh, Tolly!' protested Belle, her stormy hair all but engulfing her mockingly amorous face. 'Not before? Haven't you always loved me? Were you really so hard-hearted that you had to wait till we met before you loved me?'

Tolly begged her pardon; then, by way of apology, kissed her very formally upon the nose. To which Belle responded with a serious wrinkling of her kissed portion and an admission that, though they'd undoubtedly loved each other since the beginning of time, it was their first meeting that had given it a name. In her case, Tolly; in his, Belle.

They nodded thoughtfully, and were silent as they contemplated anew the many unique features of their love that lifted them up so high that they seemed to be travelling along, several yards in the air above the painted *Argosy*.

'Ain't they sweet?' said Mrs Hannah, the Crown Jeweller's wife. 'Mr Hannah's promised to make 'em a pair of real gold rings for when they should be married. Which will be soon, please God!'

To which prayer there was a general murmur of assent; it was perfectly plain to all that Belle and Tolly were no more to be parted than the sun from the sky.

'But the Carters may be very grand folk,' murmured Mrs

Carmody, with an air of gentle warning. 'They mayn't be eager to give their consent.'

'Not eager?' cried Dr Carmody, with a look of shining incredulity. 'Not eager, ma'am? After what that boy and I have done for her? Is it possible? Ain't they flesh and blood? And will not blood quicken and flesh melt? Their consent is but a formality. We only seek it so that they may see their lost child miraculously restored; and that she may see, once and for all, that her malady was but a passing disorder that has gone into the nothingness from which it came.'

Mrs Carmody sighed and nodded. Whatever doubts she might have had, gave way to her husband's infectious complacency. For it was already the second of October and the wagons were in harbour by Reigate.

A fine, clear morning – but with the finger of winter upon it. Though the sun was out, it provided little heat and seemed no more than a pallid memento in the sky of better days.

Tolly, Belle and Dr Carmody were dressed as handsomely as was agreeable with warmth. Mrs Carmody fluttered from one to the other, straightening cravats, brushing collars and generally settling in her own mind that there was nothing about them that the grandest family could take exception to. They were about to call upon the Carters.

Proudly she watched them on their way and even persuaded Cassandra to wave to 'the pretty lady and her fine young man' as they walked beside Papa.

As always, they were hand in hand, and, as always, there was a hint of dancing in their step. Belle's flaring yellow gown, hid under a grey cloak, peeped and tumbled out from time to time – as if excitement was too much for long concealment.

Tolly watched her sideways – could not take his eyes off her – and his face, which Mrs Carmody had always considered more homely than handsome, seemed as warm and well-furnished with affection as the best home in the land.

'God bless them,' she sighed; and Cassandra, seeing her

mother's eyes grow moist, began to sob and howl in the firm belief that all tears signified disaster.

They went to the Castle Inn where, it had been agreed, Tolly and Belle were to wait while Dr Carmody called at the mansion to prepare the Carters for the splendid surprise that awaited them.

No better ambassador could be imagined; his credentials being in his face. Dr Carmody was welcome anywhere. Tolly and Belle settled down to wait with an impatience that drew indulgent smiles from even the most disgruntled of travellers.

At first they sat on a bench by the door; then they fidgeted off to another, nearer the fire; till at last a shadowy place in the corner was vacated and they sped to it with secret smiles – as if none but they knew the value of seclusion.

Here they drank from the same side of the same tankard of mulled ale, and exchanged kisses of extraordinary neatness and brevity whenever they were sure no one was looking their way. To which end, they maintained an intent silence while their eyes flicked from customer to customer in the parlour, staring each out of countenance, till in the invisibility of dropped eyes, they were enabled to kiss again.

'Bleeding lovebirds,' mumbled the landlord. 'Anyone would think they didn't have the rest of their lives for such nonsense.'

None the less, even he was unwillingly fascinated by the skill displayed in the corner of his parlour, and dimly understood – in company with everyone else – that here was a love quite out of the ordinary slap, tickle and peck. For at one time or another, had it not befallen each of them . . . ?

Then at last, the door opened. The room grew briefly cold. The fire flinched in the grate, and began to smoke copiously.

'It's on hinges, mister. Marvellous new invention. It shuts when you pushes it,' said the landlord with heavy irony. Dr Carmody nodded, and shut the door. He was returned.

The good ambassador. Welcome anywhere. The lovers in

the corner stared at him. Even as the October sun still stood in the sky but gave no warmth, so the smiles stayed on their faces – but gave no joy.

The doctor came towards them. If his countenance had once been his fortune, it was now all spent. For the first time its light was out: it gave neither promise nor hope.

He sat down somewhat heavily. Attempted to smile; then shook his head and studied the scarred tabletop ... as if the sight of Tolly and Belle distressed him beyond measure.

'Dr Carmody –'

'My dears,' he muttered. 'I – I have bad news. Mr Carter – your father, Belle ... a week ago ... he – there was an – an accident. He – he is dead, my dear.'

The unhappy doctor was quite broken. It was as if the black bird of calamity had nested, not on his shoulder but in his own heart. Never before had his splendid face been met with so piercing a dismay. He was bewildered with the speed with which the boy had plainly guessed there was darker news yet. There was no mistaking the dread in his eyes. In vain Dr Carmody tried to avoid them. They followed him everywhere, questioning, wondering, fearing ...

'Let us go, my dears,' he murmured uneasily. 'There's nothing to be done here.'

'But my mother?' whispered Belle. 'Can I not see her?'

'Abroad. Mercifully. And your sister, too. She's married now. Some happiness there ... But nothing for you here. Everything – everything's been attended to. Lawyers, you know ...'

'His grave,' said Belle sadly – not remembering the man who was dead, but mourning him none the less. 'I ought to put flowers –'

'He's buried in London, child. In the circumstances ... some family there ... the funeral ...'

'But my – my home?'

'Come away, Belle. Come away!'

It was Tolly who spoke. His voice was low and shaking. He

136

took Belle by the arm and, looking neither to right nor left, stumbled out of the inn.

'In the circumstances.' In *what* circumstances? 'An – accident.' What accident? And what lay in that tiny pause between 'an' and 'accident'? A vile pause, no wider than a knife, but just as deadly.

He could not look at Belle. He could not speak to her. He feared she'd read the despair in his eyes, his voice ... All he could do was to hold her tightly by the hand and pray that the very substance of his fingers did not betray his terrible suspicion.

Mercifully, she seemed too wrapped in her own sorrow to sense the anguish in him.

Then, later that day, when they were home and Belle was safely out of hearing, Dr Carmody confided what Tolly had already guessed.

'The poor wretch was found with his pistol beside him. Quite by chance a physician was first there. He'd knocked on the door at the very instant of the gunshot. The healing hand knocking on one portal, so to speak, at the very moment the destroying hand knocked upon the other. A Dr Jones. Eminent man. Private madhouse in London. Respectable ... the best people. Thank God the footman recognized him. Took him at once to the tragedy. No time lost. Jones examined the – the unfortunate man. Even sent for blankets and brandy – just in case ... Behaved splendidly. But to no purpose. Life was extinct.'

The doctor paused and shook his head.

'Cleaning his gun when it went off, shall we say? Jones gave that as his opinion; and begged the household to support it. Sensible, kindly man. And professional, too. They say he was terribly shaken. Had to have some brandy himself. But he bore up. Even searched the writing table in case there was a note, you understand. Nothing. For that much, I suppose, one can be thankful. At least there's always doubt. And that was Dr Jones's opinion, even though he admitted there was a bad history. There'd been, it seemed, curious behaviour for some time past. Nervousness without cause; every sign of being persecuted, even haunted ... and then confusion of speech at his daughter's wedding (a fatal sign, that). All these were pointers, signposts. But alas! Such signposts are never read aright till the journey's run its fatal course. Unfortunately we can read them now.

'There's no possible doubt, poor Tolly, that the girl's father laid violent hands upon himself. It was the suicide of a madman.

'She must never know it, but the malady is in her very blood. For the moment, and for the moment only, it has stepped into another room of her mind. But it will return. She is still mad, Tolly; and, like her tragic father, may destroy herself.'

So it had come. The blow he'd most feared, yet most expected. For the expectation of calamity had ever been deep within him. In his heart of hearts he'd known that such happiness as he and Belle had aspired to was not to be achieved.

Dully he recalled his uncle's joyless words. 'Beware of smooth waters; they may hide the whirlpool. Beware of clear skies; for out of them may roar the whirlwind. Shun great happiness; then you may avoid great grief.'

Now the whirlwind had caught him and stung and buffeted him and broken his hopeful spirit. How long would it be before Belle was lost again? Better never to have seen her come so far into the light, than, having seen her, to watch her fall back again.

Her charm, her curious beauty, her comedy that slipped so quickly to seriousness, then back again to gentle mockery, her very smile, even ... all would crumple into madness, violence and self-destruction; or worse, would abruptly decay into a vacancy ...

Fearfully he observed her for some sign, some faint warning. What would it be? Too well he knew. The return of her strange vision. Every turn of her head, every fixing of her eyes now became a matter of uneasy suspense ... till, feeling his scrutiny, Belle would turn a gravely inquiring face upon him – when he'd respond with a smile as if nothing in the world was amiss.

Such a smile! To him, it felt as though it was nailed upon his face with spikes of iron. Then Belle would smile likewise and lay a hand on his shoulder and leave him to his reveries while she went to play with Cassandra, of whom she'd grown humorously fond.

Tolly's reveries! That he'd never leave her, he'd resolved on long ago. But he could not save himself from brooding on what he'd do when her spirits hurried into their last confusion. Or worse still; what would become of her if he should die first? He shivered and determined to keep in health, avoid all quarrels and never approach a horse from behind.

But come what may, Belle must never know. As he watched her now, his deep and abiding love was sometimes sharpened by a bitter anger at the alien tincture in her blood, and that she should carry so lightly within her the malady he'd thought was gone. But she must never know it.

These were the darkest days that Tolly had ever known; and as the *Argosy* lumbered through Surrey and into Kent – for winter was at hand – the lovers' loss of spirits seemed to spread a lowering infection from wagon to wagon, down the line. Even Mrs Arbuthnot, though her prophecy had been fulfilled, was without her customary fire. Indeed, she'd become so frightened of her own powers that she dared not raise her eyes to the night sky for fear of what the stars might show her. Thus, when Faversham was to be reached and the Carmodys were first upon the road, she could bring herself to say no more than: 'Don't nobody ask me what will happen next. Don't nobody ask me; for I daren't speak!'

But once again, as with all plagues and infections, there were some who escaped. Black Jack had watched the boy sinking under his mysterious grief. And, as he watched, his own unfathomed heart had stirred within him.

He had seen much and divined more. Black Jack could still, when he chose, move as silently as a vast cloud. This was, perhaps, his most formidable quality. Together with his un-natural size and strength, he possessed shrewdness and cunning in proportion. He was a more terrible adversary than Tolly supposed.

But to what end he meant to put the knowledge he'd gathered, there was no present telling. None the less, Jed in his wagon sensed that his mighty companion was nursing some scheme. Of an evening, the lantern light seemed to reveal, in the forests of his beard, the crooked track of a smile . . .

Then, one day, Black Jack obtained from the innocent Dr Carmody sufficient hints and unwise evasions for whatever he lacked to be supplied.

Still he bided his time, even to the middle of December: even to one sombre Sunday morning, hard by Faversham. It was a bitter, angry morning with the wind coming in fierce gusts to rip the last leaves from the trees and thence to sweep them, as if with an enormous broom, into dark and desolate corners where they danced madly, then lay cold and still.

Tolly and his master – together with other wagoners – were gone to a nearby inn to seek stabling for the horses, which were grown restive under the villainous wind.

They had been gone half an hour, and Belle was watching out for their return. Black Jack saw her. He called and beckoned. Then the wind blew fierce and flattened his hair and beard against the striking outline of his face and head. He called again. Belle nodded, put on her cloak, and went to Jed's wagon. She had no great fear of the giant. She did not think he meant her any harm . . .

Black Jack bade her sit on the couch beside him. She shook her head and remained standing. He studied her, observing intently her small, expectant face. Her eyes were singularly brilliant. He could not but marvel inwardly at what he knew.

Then he said: 'Dr Jones's madhouse in Islington. That's where you belong. You know it, don't you?'

The brilliance of her eyes grew more pronounced on account of the tears that had come into them. But her face displayed no shock or disbelief at the malevolent giant's words. Indeed, she seemed almost to have expected them.

'So I am not cured?' she whispered, but so softly that the monstrous ruffian had to lean forward to hear her. 'It was my father, wasn't it? There was something –'

'He killed himself,' said Black Jack harshly. He, like Tolly, had visited the bottom of the world; but he would rise out of it, no matter what the cost. 'His madness sprang on him. And his malady is in your blood. It will return. At any time, it will return. Then you will do as your father did. There is no hope for you.'

Tears were now running freely down her cheeks and falling on the collar of her cloak. But she continued to gaze at the giant without anger or even bitterness. This Black Jack found hard to support.

'I know there was – something he would not tell me. It – it was very sad to watch him . . . and to know that he was afraid to tell me. Perhaps I should have asked him? But I could not. I was so frightened he'd blame himself for failing to keep it from me.

'He's very strange, Black Jack, isn't he?' She smiled sadly. 'He's so defiant of his feelings . . . I expect that's his uncle, the sea-captain at work! But if only he knew how plainly and wonderfully they show at times, I – I don't know what he'd do! We both love him, don't we, Black Jack?'

Bleakly the giant stared at her.

'But your health and strength, Black Jack, are better than mine. Must I leave him, then? Must I go to – to Islington?'

'Yes. Yes. Yes! You *must* go. You say you love him? How come then, that you'd foul his life with watching and waiting till you should end your own, like your father before you? A queer love, that. And what of after? D'you think he wouldn't be haunted to his dying day by the moment when he'd turned his back and you had murdered yourself? A strange love you got, miss. A love I wouldn't care to have laid on me.'

Now Belle's face began to show some measure of her distress: But Black Jack was implacable. Perhaps he partly believed in what he said? Perhaps he'd inflicted certain wounds upon himself that bled inwardly and gave no outward sign? Such countenances as his seem made of rock, to be cracked only by an earthquake . . .

'It's a better love than that, Black Jack. I promise you, it's a love that's good enough.'

'For what?'

Her tears were halted. She frowned at her harsh opponent.

'Will you stay with him, then, Black Jack?'

Slowly the giant nodded. 'He and I have – have unfinished business. Tolly and me . . .'

'I'll not say you told me –'

'Damn you! You'll tell him – or I will! I want no favours, miss!'

'No,' said Belle bitterly. 'No more favours, that is. I'll go, Black Jack. I'll make no commotion. I'll go quietly as they say . . .'

'To the madhouse?'

'To the madhouse.'

15

'YOU vile, inhuman mountain of evil! You dreadful croaking toad! Monstrous within as you are without! Oh God! That they'd hanged you proper! Oh God! That I'd let you choke and rot in your coffin! That they'd took you off to Surgeons' Hall and chopped you into pieces to look for your heart! Or drowned you in spirits so that you'd last forever as a peep-show of what it's like in Hell! See! See! Here's one of its monsters! It looks like a man but it's not! God knows what it is –'

Thus Tolly, at the top of his distracted voice, to Black Jack who stood and watched him. Then Tolly went for the giant with a lump of wood; and Black Jack knocked him senseless. Jed took him into his wagon and rubbed his head with Elixir. Tolly recovered – then went for Black Jack again: this time with the jug, and Jed had to interpose himself to prevent the giant from killing the boy outright.

Belle was gone and Black Jack had told him why.

Cruelly early in the morning, while Tolly had slept, Dr Carmody had taken her. Black Jack had expected some sort of outburst, but even he had been taken aback by the force of it.

Jed grunted something that could have been, 'He'll get over it,' but the giant brooded uneasily. He thought he'd known the boy through and through. Maybe he had – in April. But the boy was changed. Though his rage passed, his eyes continued to burn almost feverishly. The fire that Black Jack had lit was far from doused.

Then, one afternoon, some four days later, Dr Carmody returned on Striker. The good doctor's radiant face was the very image of wisdom and peace: till he saw his apprentice.

'Where is she?'

The doctor backed away. Momentarily he feared for his safety. The boy's eyes blazed at him with a desperation at once pitiful and frightening.

'My boy ... my dear boy – it was for the best. No hope for her. Very tragic. But – but she understood. She – she begged me to take her. Could not bear to stay ... for you to wake. She loved you. You understand ... pain of parting too much for her – for you ... Begged you to forgive her and – and forget ... if possible. You must forget, dear boy. Time heals all. The horny mesentery –'

'Where did you take her?'

'No need to worry on that score! She's well looked after. Private madhouse; best of everything. Saw the proprietor. Eminent man – and honest. You see, she's being paid for ... her poor father's estate. No trouble there. Admirable matron in charge. Fine woman. Sympathetic. Works wonders, I understand. And – and they've a parson, too. Religious instruction, you know. So set your heart at rest, dear boy. Even think you've had a lucky escape! Dr Jones and I consulted together, you know. Oh yes. We made sure. Two opinions! But the father's suicide. That was it. Dr Jones agreed. Even though she seems clear (and the family, too) the suicide is the fatal speck that remains. But she'll be happy. The air is good – Islington being high up and –'

Of a sudden Dr Carmody discovered he was consoling the vacant air. His wild apprentice was gone. On the one word 'Islington', he'd cried out – and fled.

'Come back! Come back –'

But there was no voice in all the world strong enough to call him back; neither Dr Carmody's, nor Mrs Arbuthnot's nor the Crown Jeweller's, as they waved and shouted. And Black Jack stared from Jed's wagon in bleak dismay as his young saviour rushed raging to the madhouse in search of his mad love.

God or the devil knew what was in his mind during his headlong journey. Did he mean to tear Belle out of the madhouse –

or to plead on his knees with the keepers to let her go? By coach, on foot and even by vintner's cart he travelled for what must have been two days ... though it seemed to him like one immense and dreadful night in which pieces of thought blazed and fell like murdered stars.

Then, on December twenty-first, he came into Islington and found out the tall closet of a mansion in which many a family had hid its skeleton: Dr Jones's private madhouse.

He stumbled to the door and began to knock and knock and knock till his fists were bruised and near to bleeding.

'What's amiss? Who's there? Are you mad? Wait – wait!'

At last the door opened on its chain. Part of a broad face with a pelmet of faded curls peeped out.

'Belle Carter!' sobbed Tolly. 'Let me see her! For pity's sake –'

Mrs Mitchell's alarmed face softened. She smiled.

'Her fancy man,' she said. 'And come to visit. There, now, dear! Don't fret so. She's as well as any of our poor souls. Come back tomorrow, dear. Maybe you can see her then.'

She shut the door and, after Tolly had hammered on it for another full minute, she shouted, somewhat more sternly:

'Banging won't do nought but mischief, young man! Come back tomorrow, I said, and we'll see.'

None the less, he banged four or five times more and cried out 'Belle!' before he fell back from the dark door and stared up at the mansion's barred windows, hopelessly.

As he did so, he fancied something shifted behind a first floor window. Could it have been Belle, watching him? He stared and stared – but saw no more than the reflection of bare trees and a failing sky. Night was coming on ...

Inside the madhouse, a pair of sharp eyes twinkled, and a sturdy, somewhat short-legged figure resplendent in a new baize apron, nipped down to the hall from the first floor.

Hatch was in the house. Hatch was now Under-Keeper on the gentlemen's side in the departed Mitchell's place. For which elevation, he'd Dr Jones to thank. And his own quick wit.

Though he wasn't much given to looking back, he couldn't help grinning whenever he remembered Dr Jones's dismayed face in the gunpowdery parlour at Reigate when he, Hatch, had peeped out from behind the curtain and mouthed: 'Save me or we're both for it!'

White as an egg he'd gone! But one couldn't help admiring the way he'd sent the servants scuttling for blankets and brandy for all the world as if there'd still been life in tattered old Carter on the floor.

'To the coach!' he'd breathed – and Hatch winked and went.

The way everything had been covered up and attended to afterwards filled Hatch with further admiration, and a desire to learn. So when the doctor offered him Mitchell's post, he could scarce believe in his luck. 'It's an ill wind,' he murmured wonderingly. And indeed it was. Hatch, in a brand-new apron and with neat little stick, was the illest wind that had ever blown Islington way.

Every time a paper rustled or a board creaked, the parson and the doctor would look at one another, then creep to the door to see what Hatch was at. Though they hoped that one of the gentlemen inmates would stave his head in, until that happy time should come, they lived uneasily. They dared not turn him out – for Hatch knew that Mr Carter was survived by a rich widow and a daughter who'd married well.

'He wouldn't!' whispered Dr Jones; but Parson Hall smiled grimly. 'He would. Oh yes, he would. After all, our young friend Hatch, it must be admitted with shame, is only human.'

But Mrs Mitchell, tolerant soul that she was, had taken Hatch to the battlements of her bosom. She liked him and thought of him as a gay young tease.

She met him in the hall as he came down the stairs. He winked at her.

'He's still there, Mrs M. Mooning in the drive. Dangerous young 'un, that. Take my word. I know –'

'He'll soon be off, Hatch. Never you fear. It's a cold night.'

'What of when he comes again, ma'am? What of tomorrow?'

She returned his wink.

'Why bless you, you young scamp! Tomorrow never comes, do it?'

Hatch grinned.

16

January second. 1750

My dear Uncle,

I am sorry my news is no better than what I must tell you.

I am now in employment as potboy to the Angel Inn at Islington and here I must stay till – as I used to hear your sailors sing – 'the stars fall down from the sky'. I have some ties in the neighbourhood which I will never break with. I hope you are not disappointed in me, but I do promise you that a potboy – with diligence – may rise in the world and even become a landlord. (Such was the way with Mr Walker.) And on my honour, sir, I think that to keep a good house (such as ours), and dispense warmth and cheer (such as we do), is as respectable a way of getting a living as the making up of handsome clothes. Pray give my apologies to Mr Hardcastle and assure him that the circumstances in which I left him were not of his making, nor, altogether, of mine. Trusting that you are in good health, sir, and hoping to be favoured with some news of it, I remain, your respectful nephew, Bartholomew Dorking.

Tolly paused, pen in hand; crossed out 'Bartholomew' and wrote in 'Tolly'. Then he addressed the letter and gave it to his new master for dispatch. At long last, his duty was done . . .

Already a dozen tomorrows had come and gone and still the terrible matron croaked at him through the chain-held door:

'Come back tomorrow and we'll see.'

At first, he'd raged and shouted and hammered on the door; then, dreading that Belle would hear him and so be cast into a despair as deep as his own, he'd pleaded, begged even on his knees. Then he'd threatened – then instantly relented for fear reprisals would be taken on Belle – and pleaded again; only to be told:

'Come back tomorrow, dear, and we'll see.'

So he came, with the biting winds inside of his coat and the wintry sky in his heart. He brought a hamper of such delicacies as the Angel afforded; and he'd put in a letter, cunningly slipped underneath.

'Bless you,' said Mrs Mitchell moistly, spying the hamper. 'All the world loves a lover and I ain't no exception ... as poor Mitchell would testify. So just you leave the goodies on the step and come back tomorrow and we'll see what we'll see, eh?'

When he was gone, Mrs Mitchell unfastened the door and took in the hamper. She called for Hatch and went downstairs. Then she and the saucy young Under-Keeper rummaged in the basket and ate whatever was unsuited to the pale, quiet, tragic-eyed girl who was chained in the room with Polly and Sukey.

Then Hatch discovered the letter. He read it; shrugged his shoulders and passed it on to Mrs Mitchell.

'The wicked young man!' she munched as she examined it. 'To fret a poor thing with what she can't never have. Love. Ain't he wicked, Hatch?'

'Wicked,' chuckled Hatch, as Mrs Mitchell buried the letter in the tomb of her bosom.

'And she in such a bad way, too.'

Hatch looked up interestedly.

'So quiet,' went on Mrs Mitchell. 'It's the quiet ones you can't never trust. You just never know with them. You just never know –'

Here Mrs Mitchell knew what she was talking about. She'd a great long experience of not knowing. Close on thirty years of it. In her competent, assured way, she was something of an expert in ignorance ...

When Tolly returned to the inn, there was a small crowd gathered in the Angel's courtyard. They were staring up. Among them was Mr Walker, the landlord.

'What d'you think o' the sky, lad?'

'What sky, sir?'

'Is there another one, then?' asked Mr Walker seriously. 'I meant that dirty great lump of emptiness upstairs – what keeps the weather in!'

Tolly had had other matters on his mind. He'd not seen the sky for many a day now; his eyes had been fixed on the ground. For all he knew or cared, the sky could have been torn to bloody shreds. None the less he looked up.

'There!' said Mr Walker, as if he expected to be congratulated on it.

Vast and sinister curtains seemed to be hung across the heavens. Huge folds in crimson and purple that quivered as if, somewhere behind them, a great casement had been opened and a wind was stirring...

'It's the Northern Lights,' said Mr Walker, who'd once been to Scotland and never till now got any use out of it. 'But never seen in these parts before. Remarkable, ain't it?'

'It's the end of the world,' said a voice by Tolly. 'And behind them drapes waits the last Whirlwind.'

The speaker was a Guardsman, striking in scarlet and blue. His heavy face was folded into a frown.

'Ain't I seen you before?'

Tolly looked at him. He shook his head. They were strangers. Certainly, in this muscular, swelling soldier, it was hard to recognize the fallen and dazed coachman he'd once seen on the Croydon road.

But Mitchell had a better memory for faces. Only, when he'd seen Tolly before, it had been following a clump on the head. His inward state had been Apocalyptic. Thus the image of Tolly reached from one tottering condition to another ... He shuddered and hastened away.

Somewhat puzzled, Tolly watched him go till he was no more than a scarlet speck dropping down into the heap of glimmering darkness that was the Town; like a little firebrand...

The Northern Lights, the Northern Lights! Night after night they came, spreading their sombre finery across the sky. The colours and shadows and gigantic scope of them grew until they reached a terrible intensity on January twenty-third. Then slowly they faded and passed away, taking with them Tolly's wild dream that, in some way, the heavenly panoply was an omen of a good tomorrow.

How long was it now that he'd given up believing the genteel croaks that came through the chained door? He'd never given up. Each night he still believed that his tomorrow was on the other side of his present pillow. He believed there'd be a window agape; that the door would be left unchained; that Belle would be waiting for him by the wall . . .

The last of the Northern Lights was on February fourth; a pale purple shadow that hung like tattered gauze till it dwindled into nothingness as the sky forgot.

But the memory lingered in many a perilous mind.

'I hear Mr Mitchell's going great guns in the Town, Hatch,' said his lady proudly. 'Preaches regular at four chapels and a meeting-house. Real fire-eater, is Mr M when he's roused. Sounding off about whirlwinds and fire and smoke and Sodom and Gommorah and all that. Such an educated man. Wonderful, really.'

Hatch nodded. It was just before eleven o'clock in the morning and it was time for Mrs Mitchell to fetch out the brandy she'd taken off the upstairs' brandy-merchants.

'A great man, the Guardsman,' he said.

Mrs Mitchell went to her cupboard and unlocked it.

'I miss him, Hatch. I miss him sorely.'

'Who could blame you, ma'am?'

She fetched out the bottle and a pair of glasses and put them on the table.

'He'll go far, Hatch. It's not for me to hold –'

She stopped. The brandy bottle and the glasses had begun to dance and rattle in the most extraordinary fashion. Then, of

a sudden, there was a roaring in the air, as of distant gunfire. Mrs Mitchell swayed, staggered; Hatch cried out. The house, the whole tall solid house seemed suddenly on vast chains hung to the sky. It swayed ... back and forth; twice. Then it settled back on its foundations.

'What was it? What's happened?'

Mrs Mitchell mopped her brow with her apron. She took a large measure of brandy.

'D'you know what, Hatch? I think it was an earthquake!

An earthquake, Hatch! Lord! Mr M will be in his element, now! It's what he's always wanted. I tell you, Hatch, if I wasn't a God-fearing, religious woman, I'd say the Almighty had listened to Mitchell!'

Now there came a wild knocking on the front door.

'It's him,' muttered Hatch. 'Tolly. I'd know his banging anywhere.'

They sat and listened while between the banging came a frantic voice crying:

'Belle! Belle! Are you all right?'

Mrs Mitchell finished her brandy and went upstairs. She opened the door to all of its chain. Tolly's pale and terrified face stared into her calm one.

'Of course she's all right, dear. What's an earthquake to the likes of her? It'll take the end of the world to shake *our* ladies and gentlemen! So you go off and come back tomorrow; and then maybe we'll see!'

Though the earthquake had not done much for the lost souls in the madhouse and had done no injury anywhere – above a broken arm in Spitalfields – it had provoked much uneasiness in the Town. Buildings and consciences alike were searched for cracks and flaws – there having broke out a general dread that the Almighty couldn't be trusted not to strike again.

Mitchell went greater guns than ever and drew handsome congregations to hear his warnings ... to the pleasure and pride of his lady in distant Islington.

Then, little by little, even as the Northern Lights had faded from the sky, so the terrified memory of the earth's eerie motion faded from minds. The Almighty went back into Heaven where He belonged; congregations shrank and forsaken Mitchell shouted in the echoing chapels – a voice in the wilderness.

Now the Islington potboy grew sadly cunning. Twice, he'd waylaid Dr Jones, and once, Parson Hall. But they'd proved no more amiable than the matron. Indeed, the parson had threatened him with the Justice if he didn't make off and leave the madhouse in peace.

So he haunted the shadows by the gate till Mrs Mitchell should come out, when he was resolved to attack her and force her to take him back inside. But she never came ... or never, at least, till after he'd gone back to the Angel to earn his keep. Sharp eyes from a first floor window kept too close a watch for the success of anything the potboy attempted.

But Tolly, in the deepest, quietest part of his soul, had found a determination that nothing would quench – save the end of the world itself. Though there were times when he believed the hand of God was against him, and times when he fancied he was going mad with despair, he still plotted and planned strange, unlucky adventures to free his heart's desire. Till March seventh when an idea of astonishing daring came to him.

He'd stolen a washing basket from the inn: a great battered object that reeked of ancient sheets. And in the same way, he'd come by several sausages, two old loaves and a quantity of large smoked fish. With immense cunning, he escaped from the Angel at nightfall, taking the hamper of aged goodies out of the stables where he'd hid it and where, already, horses had been making free with it.

He reached the madhouse and waited till the last of its lights was doused. Then he laid the basket on the step and crouched down inside it, tumbling the delicacies over his bent head and shoulders so that, to a careless eye, there was nought within but food. Now he drew down the lid and held it firm. Upon it, painted clear, was 'Belle Carter'. When morning came, they'd open the door and take him in.

Of this he was so entirely convinced that the abominable stench that inhabited the basket seemed to him as fragrant as roses. He waited.

It was a dark and heavy night. A restless plague of a night, full of aches and startings-up and faint cries ... But the washing basket on the madhouse step stayed quiet and motionless.

Tolly, half waking, half dozing and aching in every joint and muscle he owned, bided his time. Now he peered through the ragged cane-work, now he stared into the hopeless eye of a smoked fish that had fallen against his cheek, now he closed his eyes altogether . . . and now, at last, he fell asleep.

They were moving him! He awoke. It was still dark. But the basket was being lifted – swung in air! Then – then came a terrible blow like a kick of a gigantic boot!

At exactly the same time – which was half after five in the morning, a waterman, lying but half awake in his boat at Kingston, felt a violent blow at the underside of his craft – as if some huge, malevolent fish had risen sharply. Then the river round about sprang into a commotion, tossing tethered barges and vessels into a wild confusion.

In the fields, sheep began to hurry in all directions; rooks rose screaming from trees that had begun to tremble; and from abruptly agitated ponds, fish leaped to perish on the banks. And there was a sound in the air as of distant gunfire . . .

In the drowsy Town, for a second time buildings rocked – some four or five times back and forth – tumbling china and hearts, but killing no one. But most disquieting of all, the perverse motion set great church bells on the tremble so that they gave out deep murmurs like the forewarning of a knell.

Feet stumbled over the madhouse floors. Voices shouted; among them was one of triumphant power. Mitchell was there – visiting with his yielding wife.

He rushed to a window to see how much of the world remained. Then he glimpsed a sight that thrilled his blood.

In the dark drive (where he'd been flung by the earthquake's shock), was the boy he'd seen when the Curtains of Judgement had appeared in the sky; the visionary potboy whose appearance foretold calamity.

'It's him!' whispered Mitchell. Then Tolly, dragging his broken basket, fled.

'Mitchell! My Mitchell! Must you go?' cried his lady, for the Guardsman was dressing with terrible haste.

He turned to her and she saw, of a sudden, that he was become great. 'His eyes,' she afterwards said, 'were burning. Burning like real wax candles!'

'They can't want you now!'

'I *must* go,' said Mitchell. 'There's not much time.'

'But it ain't six o'clock, dear –'

Then he answered in a voice that trembled.

'Mrs Mitchell. Make your peace with Heaven. Soon we are all to be judged.'

'How soon, dear?'

'What day is today?'

'March eight, of course –'

'We have eight and twenty days more, ma'am.' He did up the last button of his scarlet jacket. 'Which brings us to April five.'

Mrs Mitchell regarded the glittering Guardsman with a mixture of longing and wonderment.

'How so, Mitchell, dear?'

'The first touch of God's finger on this sinful Town was on February eight. The second falls on March eight. There will be a third. It will be eight and twenty days hence. Nor will it be a touch. It will be the blow of His fist. It will be the end.'

He dusted his breeches.

'So when will you come again, Mitchell? When will I see you next?'

'I've work to do, ma'am. Much, much work! Pray, ma'am. Pray hard – and maybe we'll meet in Heaven on April five.'

With that, he left her and she watched him striding off into the lifting shadows, his scarlet back as broad as a furnace door.

'April five ... April five ...' he muttered as he went; then he looked up to the mysterious sky.

'Oh God, I thank Thee for making even such as me Thy terrible prophet!'

Later that morning, Tolly, much bruised and smelling strongly, returned to the madhouse. He kicked a pair of sausages into the bushes, then peered forlornly up at the calm walls and bland windows. Neither cracks nor rents showed in its structure. He sighed. If the hand of God had failed to break in, what chance had a potboy? He knocked. Came Mrs Mitchell with a bewildered, almost feminine air.

'When is it to be?' he begged despairingly.

'April five,' said Mrs Mitchell absently. April five was much on her mind. Her husband's talk of Heaven had quite unsettled her. Could he, in his queer way, have meant hare and oysters at Clapham and a tumble in the hay?

'April five, ma'am?' repeated Tolly, scarce believing his ears.

Mrs Mitchell smiled fatly.

'April five?' At last, at last he'd been given a day! No more tomorrows! A real day!

Abruptly Mrs Mitchell came to herself. Understood what she'd said. Bit her lip. Frowned. Her word being law, she'd not openly go back on it.

'April five I said – and April five I mean. In the morning. At ten. You can see her for an hour. Now – be off with you!'

Tolly's progress back to the Angel was striking in the extreme. He danced, he hopped, he skipped and even sang. Passers by fancied the earthquake had turned his brain; but even the sourest had to grant that it had been turned to face the sun.

The landlord greeted him sternly.

'Been at the spirits, Tolly?'

'No, sir.'

'Then what's got into you, boy?'

'April five, sir. It's fair blazing inside of me like a pint of stars!'

The landlord shrugged his shoulders. It was plain he'd get no more sense out of the lad at the moment.

'Well – there's a letter come for you. Let's hope it don't put out that blaze. We could do with a cheerful potboy when there's earthquakes about!'

He gave Tolly the letter. It smelled of the sea and of snuff. It was from his uncle, the sea-captain. Tolly smiled. Another world from which he'd long since sailed away . . .

Nephew; received yours of Jan. 2. Much obliged. But must own am somewhat disappointed. After all that has been done for you, etcetera, now a potboy. Poor return. But am still your uncle and drowned father's brother, etcetera. Therefore will be pleased to see you. Strong storms round coast have laid low many fine ships. Hence am in demand. Busy. But weather, tides and God willing, will be lying in Greenwich between April 4 and 5. Ship is *The Philosopher* (figurehead, a bearded Sage and Compasses). Refitted thirty gunner with Spanish work about poop. Have conveyed yr. apologies to Mr Hardcastle. Deep regret. Yr. Affectionate uncle, Capn Dorking. Post. Script. My housekeeper begs to be remembered and was sorry you had not done the same.

Tolly laughed softly. 'My dear uncle – the sea-captain! Greenwich, April five, indeed! No offence in the world, sir, but you're a lifetime too late! I've other plans . . . such plans! Change 'em? No, sir. Not even if the end of the world was to come!'

17

'THEY'VE made my Mitchell a corporal!' said his lady to Hatch, with supernatural pride. 'It shows they believe in him. Lord above! There's no telling where he'll end up!'

Mrs Mitchell had every cause for pride. Corporal Mitchell was indeed believed. He was inspired. There was no doubt of it. The burning in his eyes, that Mrs Mitchell had observed, was mightily increased. The congregations that had fallen away, streamed and crowded back ... even fought for a near place when the terrible Corporal preached.

'Repent! Repent before the Whirlwind sweeps us all to Judgement! Two warnings have ye been sent. A third time cometh – on April five!'

Spellbound, the congregations stared up at the extraordinary prophet, heroic in scarlet and new white shoulder knots.

Then fear began to eat and gnaw away at them, like some fatal disease which spread and spread by invisible infection.

'On your knees!' shouted the Corporal, from higher and higher pulpits. 'The great wind comes! Fire and smoke even as it was with Gomorrah! Pray! Repent!'

Though it's certain that, here and there, he provoked a touch of repentance and a wisp of prayer, far and away his grandest achievement was a strange movement in the whole uneasy Town. A shifting, a stirring as of some huge blind beast fumbling for air ...

Families were moving. Whole families with their plate, linen, servants, paintings, even furniture. Carts piled like tawdry mountains, coaches and carriages tight with pale humanity, choked the narrow streets. And where the ways were wider, there was movement ... steady, groaning movement, great wheeled rivers flowed ... six hundred, even a thousand carriages in a single day on a single road. And there were many roads ...

'Repent your sins!' roared the Corporal. 'Ye have but nine days before the Whirlwind sweeps us all to Judgement!'

But the mighty tide flowed on out of the Town to seek the safety of high places, away from the peril of toppling buildings. And all the while, the price of lodgings in secure villages mounted arrogantly and offered sanctuary to the trembling rich. Which seemed, at least, the next best thing to repentance.

'There's no escape anywhere!' raged the Corporal. 'God's fist lies over all!'

'They'll make him Pope or Archbishop before he's done,' declared Mrs Mitchell in Islington, awed beyond measure by her husband's outstanding success. 'There's no telling *how* high he'll go!'

'Eight ... seven ... six more days to save your wretched souls!' bellowed the Corporal, telling off the days to his day of fire and grand calamity.

'Five more days ... four more days...' whispered the potboy in Islington, telling off the days to his hour with his sweetheart chained in the madhouse.

'Will you really let him in on Thursday?' asked Hatch uneasily; for he saw no profit in another meeting with Tolly.

'Bless you, dear,' said Mrs Mitchell. 'Of course I won't! The idea!'

'Then –'

'Don't bother me now, Hatch. I'm a-dreaming on my wonderful Corporal.'

She smiled radiantly and settled back in her chair ...

'Repent! Even now there's time!' shrieked the possessed Corporal, sweeping all before him like mad leaves before a mad broom. 'Three more days for –'

Abruptly the Corporal's voice was stilled. He'd reached the top of his mountain. The black winds blew round him everywhere.

He was took and flung urgently into Bedlam. But it was no

remedy. Confining the madman could not halt the passage of the days. Time shrank, drew into its shell like the Snail of the Universe, tottering into its grave. Three ... two ... one.

Now up out of the doomed Town crept its queer dregs. It was as if the dark conglomeration of lanes, alleys, churches, tenements and mansions was already on the tremble and these uncanny sooty gentry with their bulbous carts and bending nags had come out of newly opened places in the ground.

Though they were but the sweeps and tinkers and street-vendors, they might have been demons ... Up, up, up the long hill into Islington they came, from this last day's dawn till past four o'clock.

Already the sun was deep and bloody and had a deathbed droop. All the glasses and tankards and walls in the Angel's parlour were touched with its scarlet, and the shadows seemed as deep as gaping rents in the ground.

Slowly the dregs of the Town trudged and trundled past the windows, seeking shelter against the coming storm. But everywhere was full – full to bursting with those who'd come before.

Stranger and wilder grew the sights in the road outside the Angel as the watchers in the parlour stared. Then –

'My God! What's that?'

'Hell's opened up this time!'

'What a thing! What a creature! The size of it!'

'Merciful Heavens! Pistols, quick! It's coming this way!'

The parlour door opened.

'I'm looking for a lad called Tolly Dorking,' said Black Jack.

'Been here all the time?' grunted Black Jack, when Tolly had been fetched from the cellar and, to everyone's relief, had led the hellish monster outside.

'Working as a potboy, Black Jack.'

Tolly smiled with pleasure as he saw Jed's wagon halted nearby. At last it had broken free from the *Argosy*.

'I ain't asking forgiveness. I ain't come for that,' said Black Jack harshly.

'No, Black Jack. I didn't suppose you had. But I'm pleased to see you –'

Black Jack sneered incredulously. Tolly bit his lip angrily. Then his intense happiness on his coming hour with Belle got the better of him. He confided his news to Black Jack; and could not keep the triumph out of his face and voice.

Black Jack stared at his young saviour in amazement. He saw the months had dealt unkindly with the boy; his thinned-out face had an almost feverish flush of expectancy. The giant screwed up his features into all the furrows of a stormy sea.

'All for an hour? Jed!' he shouted. 'Look! He's a potboy now! All these weeks and weeks for an hour! What d'you think o' that, Jed?'

Jed appeared and nodded as if he thought a great deal but wouldn't say it. Then Black Jack put his hands on Tolly's shoulders so that the boy almost sank under their weight.

'Not in your full health and strength, eh?'

He peered intently into Tolly's eyes.

'Enough to see me through!' said Tolly indignantly ... and wished he could halt his tears. But the enormous face that stared so closely into his own seemed to suck them out of his eyes. At last in that vast countenance was the look he'd once have given his soul to have seen. Black Jack was staring at him in admiration.

Abruptly the giant freed the boy. 'Wait here!' he muttered.

'Where are you going?'

'To fetch her forth. From the madhouse.'

Tolly looked at him in terror. All would be ruined! Once again the monster would cross him. His precious hour would be lost!

'No! Don't, Black Jack! Don't –'

But Black Jack was on his way, striding like some ferocious monk off to do battle with the devil.

'I'm in me full health and strength, Tolly!' he snarled, as

the boy sought to hold him back. 'What I done, I can undo. There ain't no living soul to stand against me. Keep your distance, boy! I'm out of your reaching. I'm face to face with me Maker, Tolly –'

'Then – who was it made you ... Black Jack?'

The giant scowled. 'A man and a woman – just like you, boy. Only they was cast-offs. He went on the rope; and she was quick with me ... for which she was spared. But not for long. I did for her when I was born. No escape for the cast-offs. Till now, Tolly. For I'm rising up in me health and strength. I'm presenting me account, Tolly. I ain't no chapel bankrupt. I'm rising up – and God help him what tries to keep me down!'

In the peaceful madhouse, Mrs Mitchell sat in her parlour, nibbling her pen and composing a melancholy letter to the Colonel of her husband's regiment. 'My Lord, he is not mad now; if your Lordship would but get any *sensible* man to examine him, he would find he is quite in his right mind –'

Suddenly there came a tremendous loud banging at the front door.

'Hatch!' she shouted. 'Go see who's there!'

She resumed her letter. 'The business of the Whirlwind is Mr Mitchell's only maggot. And that, I do swear, is from being plagued with wind since infancy so it has got to his head. So I beg you, my Lord, to free my dear Mitchell from horrid Bedlam –'

Here she was interrupted again; this time by a loud cracking then a scream to which was attached several dismayed groans.

'Drat him!' muttered Mrs Mitchell. 'What's he up to now with his gentlemen? Oh he's a rascally little tease with that stick of his!'

Now came other noises and Mrs Mitchell dropped her pen and hastened up to the hall.

'God preserve us!'

The heavy door chain was snapped and the dingy hallway

was full of a stinking, black-bearded ruffian in monk-like rags! Behind him, half hid by his huge bulk, was the love-mad potboy.

'God preserve us!' said Mrs Mitchell again. She saw the aproned Hatch.

He was fallen back against the stairs. He was, as she afterwards said, 'all of a terrible tremble with knees and teeth chattering like milk churns . . .'

'It's the ten pound – that's what you come for, ain't it?' gabbled Hatch desperately. 'Was just going to send it! 'Mazing! Fetch it directly! Word of honour . . . Ten pound on the nail, Mister Jack . . . God's –'

But whatever quality of the Almighty was on the tip of Hatch's tongue to mention, remained mysterious. The monster, having recovered from his astonishment on meeting with the treacherous Hatch, moved with wonderful speed. ('Considering his bulk,' recalled Mrs Mitchell, 'his motions were something tremendous – like them sea-birds what pounce; only he was black – black as sin.')

Hatch screeched. Black Jack had him by the throat and was shaking him so that it was a marvel his head didn't fly off.

'Where's the girl?' snarled the great brute. 'Tell me – or I'll pound you into mud!'

On which Mrs Mitchell shrieked 'Murder!' and bolted for the doctor and the parson.

Then the tall closet of a mansion broke out into a clamour of dismay. The matron's shriek, echoing in all the sad rooms, provoked such a panic as only a madhouse can know. Shouts and screams and curses and the banging of chains told of dreadful notions and attempts to escape whatever the iron matron had screamed at.

Sweat broke out on Black Jack's brow. Dirty rivulets of it ran down and into his beard. His eyes glittered. He licked at his dried-up lips . . .

Hatch, with his neck half broke, saw Black Jack's face dancing before him. He saw the giant's rage beginning to fail as his old fears rose. Hatch choked out: 'Mad! She's mad! Screams and foams at the chops! Mad like her pa! Ain't you heard? Killed himself! In her blood! Leave her! Can't have her –'

Even in his present extremity, Hatch had a mind to protect his investment.

The screams and shrieks dinned in the giant's ears. He faltered; staggered; let Hatch fall. The Under-Keeper scrambled half-way up the stairs, from which high place he turned and jeered: 'Mad! Mad! The house is full of it! All like her! Raving! Horrible! Waiting to get you, Black Jack! Hark at 'em!'

Bewildered, Black Jack turned about. For Tolly? Tolly was gone! Dismay seized the huge man. He was alone. Tolly had left him alone with his darkest fear...

Then, over and above the madhouse clamour, came Tolly's voice.

'She's here! Black Jack – I've found her!'

In that infernal uproar, Tolly had heard Belle! And had run as he'd never run in his life before. Door after door he'd shouted at, getting answers as wild as the wind, till at last had come the one he longed for. But the door was locked. He needed Black Jack's health and strength.

Black Jack moved. Hatch screamed violently: 'Leave her! She's ours!'

'Lord be praised! Hatch has been spared!'

Mrs Mitchell, the doctor and the parson were arrived. Black Jack glared savagely at them.

'We must be calm ... we must be peaceable ... we must be quiet ...' muttered the doctor from habit.

'Calm? Spared?' shouted Hatch – mad for praise on his triumph. '*I* stopped him! *I* scared the living daylights out of him! Ha-ha! I told him about her pa! About old Carter –'

'You damned little fool!' raged impulsive Dr Jones, glaring at his Under-Keeper and quite misunderstanding him. 'D'you want us all hanged?'

'No! No!' screamed Hatch, outraged and panic-stricken. 'I told him it was suicide! I never said more! I never said –'

He stopped. Terrible looks were exchanged. The giant's eyes widened. His great fists clenched. Hatch made wretched attempts to undo the damage he'd done himself.

'Suicide . . . suicide . . . dead and buried now. All over with. Buried . . .'

'Buried,' repeated Dr Jones soothingly – and hoped the savage fellow hadn't understood.

But Parson Hall was not deceived. His eyes, ever-burning and prophetical on account of a malformation of the lids, sought out the giant's soul. He grew pale . . .

'Black Jack!' came Tolly's urgent voice. But Black Jack shook his head. There was a greater urgency now.

'Where – is – he – buried?'

The madhouse guardians stared at the giant in dread as they understood what he was intending.

'It – it's months! There'd be nought left to see. That is, even supposing –'

'Where is he buried?'

'Would you raise the dead?' muttered the parson desperately. 'Oh, you are damned indeed!'

'*Where is he buried?*'

'What can he find now? It don't signify –'

'Not at Tyburn!' cried Mitchell of a sudden, knowing nothing of the terrible undercurrents and only wanting her hall to be cleared. 'You murderous great pig, you! Nor in quicklime at Christchurch, neither! He's buried good and respectable at Old Street – and long may he rest till Judgement –'

'Black Jack! Black Jack!'

'Scoundrel!' shouted the parson as the giant lumbered after Tolly's cry. 'Would you interfere with them whom God has cursed? Would you set yourself against the Almighty?'

But Black Jack had gone from the hallway and the next that was heard of him – in the midst of the ceaseless shouts and shrieks of Dr Jones's ladies and gentlemen – was the crash of his shoulder bursting through a locked door. Then came Tolly's mighty shout of joy that set the madhouse ringing.

Her yellow gown was torn and fouled; her hair was lank from lack of care; her eyes seemed to have grown at the expense of her face ... yet she was still Belle. 'If I'd known I was to see you I would have tidied – I would have –'

'Belle!' wept Tolly. 'Come away from this dreadful place!'

She stared at him, then lifted the hem of her gown. Tolly saw the stout, sensible anklet and chain that Belle, wretchedly ashamed, had hid from his first sight. Tears of anguish filled his eyes. He turned to the giant who'd held back in silence from this strangest of lovers' meetings.

Black Jack nodded. He knelt and grasped the chain where it was secured to the wall.

'No! No!' moaned Belle. 'Leave me here! I'm mad – mad!'

Black Jack began to heave. The veins in his neck swelled out like ropes. The madhouse guardians cried out and shook their fists from the broken doorway; but dared not venture further.

Again Black Jack strained – and the chain gave up its anchorage. Pieces of brick, rotting wood and such a quantity of dust came out of the broken wall that it seemed the house was done for.

'No – no!' screamed Belle. 'I'll not go!'

'Ruffians! Thieves! Madmen!' shouted Mrs Mitchell, and went at the wild potboy with her powerful arms tilted like a mainyard.

'Tomorrow!' muttered Tolly vengefully. 'Come back tomorrow and we'll see!'

Down went his head as she came. He met her in mid-career. Struck her amidships, between poop and forecastle and felt her iron-work bend. She grunted. Cried out 'Hatch! Hatch!' four or five times – then struck her colour and went down.

Black Jack was dragging at Belle; seemed to be spending

much strength on so frail a thing ... for she clung and clutched at the wall, the floor, items of bedding, anything ...

'Leave me here! I'm mad! I'll kill myself like my father! Leave me!'

She shook her head till her ragged hair flew and lay across her face like a tattered shroud.

'Hatch! Hatch!' shouted the parson and the doctor. More cautious than their sunken matron, they backed away and roared for assistance. But Hatch did not come ...

Now they were in the hallway and Tolly sized hold on Belle more fiercely than the giant had dared.

'Tolly!' she moaned. 'I love you – I love you – and that's why! Leave me here ... for pity's sake, don't make me be a burden to you! The madness ... will come again!'

'Hatch, come help us!' Mrs Mitchell, breathing brokenly, clutched a banister for support.

'I'm hopeful – hopeless!' wailed Belle, holding now to the door of her terrible sanctuary.

'You're alive!' Furiously Tolly pulled her free. 'That's enough! While there's life, there's always hope!'

'And likewise, while there's death!' snarled Black Jack at the madhouse guardians.

'Satan!' hissed Parson Hall.

'Hatch!' croaked Mrs Mitchell, as she watched the wild visitors heave out and into the air. 'Where have you got to, Hatch?'

Hatch was upstairs in a formidable mood. He was among his shackled gentlemen. They were unlocked. He was prodding and poking and even cautiously kicking them.

'Go to it, you mad lot!' he raged. 'Go to it and tear 'em to pieces! Bite 'em – scratch 'em – strangle 'em!'

He'd found an old chopper – a rust-bitten object from the kitchen. He laid it temptingly on the floor.

'Here's something nice! Make mincemeat ... chop – chop!' But the madmen stared at him dully, and never stirred from their loosed chains.

'You, pa! You was a butcher, once! Don't it stir your blood? Mincemeat?'

He poked an aged fellow with large, yellowed hands. 'Go on! After 'em! Chop – chop!'

The old man gave a sudden squeal of pain.

'Let's go!' shouted Hatch. The old man had seized his stick.

Hatch backed to the door. His anger turned to alarm.

'Keep away! You won't get no supper –'

The old man was on the move.

'I'll – I'll get Dr Jones to put you back in the strait-weskitt!'

But Hatch's threats made no mark. Indeed, very little made any mark on this old man. Day and night themselves scarce reached into his shrouded mind ... and seemed but one darkness followed by another, darker still. Yet there was one fragment of knowledge that stuck fast. He still knew the difference between kindness and cruelty; in which he had the advantage of Hatch.

'Keep off! Keep off!'

Hatch was going down the stairs wonderfully quick on account of the crazy old wretch being after him with the chopper.

'Save me!' yelled Hatch, seeing the doctor, the parson and Mrs Mitchell in the hall. But they seemed petrified.

'He'll kill me!' howled Hatch, and bolted through the open door. Whereupon his aged pursuer gave what he supposed to be a terrible roar but which came out as a quavering shriek, and tottered after him.

'The Almighty works in mysterious ways,' whispered the awed parson, 'His vengeance to perform.'

Hatch was fumbling at the gate. Nearer came the madman with his chopper ...

'I can't bear it!' moaned Mrs Mitchell, hiding her face in her apron. 'The poor young soul!'

Hatch was through the gate and running. After him went the madman. But, in the very nature of things, the old man was ... old. Though his spirit was kindled, his limbs were burnt out. He collapsed outside the gate and could do no more than wave his chopper after the departing Hatch.

'The Lord be praised!' cried Mrs Mitchell. 'Hatch has been spared again!'

Dr Jones hurried out to fetch the old man back while Parson Hall shook his head.

'It makes one lose faith,' he muttered sourly, 'in Divine Vengeance altogether.'

18

BELLE crouched in the back of the wagon and stared at her saviours with huge, unhappy eyes. Why had they come like thunder to waken her again? What were they going to do with her? What had Black Jack meant by 'while there's death, there's hope'? And what had he and Tolly been whispering, so wild and desperate, with many a sidelong glance to her?

She felt sick at heart and believed her malady to be creeping once more through her veins and seeking out her head.

Suddenly the wagon halted. Jed shouted out: 'It's close at hand!'

Black Jack and Tolly seized hold of a spade each.

'Shall I wait?' asked Jed.

'No,' said Tolly. 'At Greenwich. There's a ship called *The Philosopher*. Spanish work about the poop. You and Belle wait for us there!'

Belle stared. Momentarily her spirit flickered.

'It – it's not him, Tolly? Not your uncle, the sea-captain?'

She smiled – and Tolly looked briefly offended. Then she looked contrite. 'Where are you going now?'

Tolly stared at her. Shook his head.

'Where are you going?' she asked Black Jack with sudden fear.

The giant scowled. 'To raise up the dead.'

The world was drawing to its end. By six o'clock the clouds were come up from the east in wild prophetical shapes: toppling buildings, touched with fire from the falling sun. There was St Paul's, there the Monument and there the crumbly Abbey, torn to slowly flaming wisps...

A man in Brick Lane was selling pills against the earthquake.

'Five shillings the box! Very powerful agin' the cramps and griping. Here, sir . . . here, ma'am! Earthquake pills!'

A sleek, fat little fellow in a moleskin hat who nosed the air as if he'd just come up out of the ground . . .

Late leavers, who'd stayed till this last of possible days, hastened by him so that he had to hurry alongside to complete his business: no one was disposed to tarry in the doomed and darkening streets.

Yet there were still some who'd resolved to stay. They jeered out of upper windows at the folly below. But from these same bold houses, children crept forth – quietly sent by the scoffers – and ran after the man in the moleskin hat, begging his pills for even ten shillings the box.

'Five shillings the box! Five shillings – who'll buy? You, young man? You, brother – Gawd Almighty!'

He'd plucked at a mad and terrible pair. A giant monk and a

wild-eyed potboy! What a sight, under the tottering sky –
hurrying, hurrying, with spades on their shoulders, pushing all
aside . . .

The pill-seller bent to pick up the boxes that had been
knocked from his hand. He looked back. He saw the huge man
hoist the potboy up and over the railings of St John's Church-
yard. Then the giant followed. His spade stood against the sky
like a great, dark axe; then he and the boy vanished among the
tilting stonework. The pill-seller grew pale, and hurried elsewhere for fear of what the graveyard might soon cast forth.

*

He lay with many Carters – a most quiet and proper family,
all under the same green quilt. Here was an uncle who'd died
of an ague; there, an aunt who, in her eightieth year, had been
taken off by a chill. God rested their souls; together with the
souls of Solomon Carter, Eliza Carter, Jacob Carter and
William Carter, aged seven.

But David Carter – tragically in his sixty-third year . . .
whom God had forgiven, was not to be left to rest.

A huge spade struck and tore the green quilt above him . . .
then another. Again and again the spades struck, till the earth
flew up in gusts and scudding showers, spattering the stones
and spoiling the green. Bending above these spades, were two
questing faces: one enormous, bearded, black as sin – the
other young, desperate, not knowing nor daring to know what
lay beneath . . . only wild with hurry. For the day was going
and there was a ship at Greenwich and a wagon lumbering to
meet it . . .

No words passed between them; all had been said. They
saved their breath for their digging, and quick and harsh it
came.

Suddenly they were interrupted. The sexton had spied them
from the church porch. Lantern in hand, he glimmered round
the stones and monuments.

'Monsters! Blasphemers! What –'

Even as he shouted, there came the sound of a spade striking on wood. The coffin had been reached. The sexton groaned in dismay. The great, monk-like ruffian was crouched down in the grave like some villainous mockery of stone respect, scraping and clawing the earth from the coffin lid. And the boy stood over him, panting and glaring with sweaty desperation.

'Blasphemers!' muttered the sexton, half frightened for his soul. He made to go, but the monster in the grave grunted: 'Keep with us! The lantern. We'll have need of it. Stay – or I'll smash you into the earth!'

Now he forced his spade under the coffin lid and began to heave it up. The screws groaned as they left their anchorage; then the spade's handle was halted by the heaped up earth.

'My Gawd! Not with his bare hands?' whispered the sexton.

Black Jack's fingers were in the gaping wood. Slowly, slowly, he forced the dismal box to open. The sexton shuddered; Tolly cried out – and Black Jack roared in a voice that would surely have waked the dead man if –

'Where is he? Where's he been took?'

Black, vacant . . . untenanted: the coffin was empty!

The sexton trembled so violently that the adjacent tombs twitched and danced as if they were troubled by unquiet slumbers below.

'I'm innocent!' he moaned. 'He was coffined proper! The undertakers. They know it. Ask them. For Gawd's sake, ask them! Corner of Brick Lane. Just yonder. They'll know!'

The Undertakers. Discreet house; windows lined with black – as if they were mourning cards in which each passer-by might see his own face. Funerals furnished for the Nobility and Gentry. Terms moderate. Discretion and Dignity. Skimpole and Gorgandy . . .

Deep in her candled parlour, sat the one-time Tyburn widow. Prosperous in black bombazeen, dreaming, perhaps, of Seven Blackfriars Lane, smiling, perhaps, on the bad old days and shillings for Mr Ketch, sighing, perhaps, on –

'A-ah!'

Mrs Gorgandy had screamed.

'Oh my Gawd! Oh my Gawd! 'Eaven forgive me! Poor, miserable sinner that I been!'

Black Jack stood before her. The great hanged monster himself. And the treacherous youth she'd left him with, nearly twelve month ago. Never, never had she forgotten them. And now they were come again. This, together with the gloomy foreboding that hung upon the Town, convinced her beyond all reasonable doubt that the world had come to its end and Judgement was at hand.

'Oh, take pity on a poor widder!'

She peered wildly past him. 'There – there ain't more of you? Oh Gawd! What if the others come? Was there any others? I mean – when you came up, sir ... was woke, so to speak ... was there many acquaintances round about – coming up, I mean – oh Gawd!'

Mrs Gorgandy's terrific notion was past her powers of expression.

'Hurry ... hurry ...' muttered the boy; and Mrs Gorgandy moaned on unthinkable prospects.

'Carter,' muttered Black Jack, with a look that seemed to promise an eternity of dismay. 'Where's he gone? Where did you sell him? Carter of Reigate –'

'Hurry ... hurry ...'

Bewilderment contended with terror in Mrs Gorgandy's brain. She stared at the youth whose bright kind eyes had once so deceived her. They would not do so again. They burned most urgently into her soul; and their fire had plainly been kindled at some blaze Mrs Gorgandy could only guess at. If he wasn't dead, he was mad ...

'*Where is he?*'

The resurrected monster pushed his great hanged face close. Lord! He stank! Which, in the circumstances, wasn't surprising. If cleanliness was next to Godliness, then Black Jack had surely come the other way.

'Them 'orrible physicians in Warwick Lane!' gabbled Mrs Gorgandy, anxious to share damnation with her customers. 'Blame them! 'Twas their wicked tempting what did it! No respect – no feeling! Ten pound for a dear departed! Oh what could a mint-new widder do? 'Eaven forgive me for taking their blood money! Spare me! Take pity! I'm a widder –'

Now began the most solemn time of Mrs Gorgandy's whole life. Black Jack reached over her table and lifted her as if she'd been no more than bombazeen and air. Then, moaning and weeping, with her violet stockinged feet scarce touching the ground, she was dragged from her house and hurried through street after street towards Warwick Lane.

Vague, troubled groups passed by on the way; queer families with link-boys flaming their ways – for the sky was vanished and a heavy blanket lay aloft. Very weird were these hastening fire-lit folk ... and Mrs Gorgandy shuddered as Warwick Lane drew near and striking notions entered her head of a Resurrection in the College of Physicians with elegantly dissected fragments laying hard claim on her ...

Now, huge and ghostly, reared St Paul's, all clustered about with link-boys thick as fireflies and a great murmuring crowd that surged up the steps ... like a vision of the Last Judgement with wigged and bonneted souls struggling for salvation, but spilling down, down among the wicked, flaming torches below.

Here, among these damned, ran the man in the moleskin hat.

'Pills against the earthquake! If you can't get in to hear the Bishop, buy my pills! Five Shillings the box! Who'll –'

Suddenly he saw, bearing down on him once more, the uncanny graveyard pair. They were haunting him. He backed away. Too late. He cursed and bent down to pick up his scattered wares. Then he hastened elsewhere ...

'Save me! Save me!' wept Mrs Gorgandy; but the cry was a commonplace about the Church and she was dragged in terror to the shabby darkness of Warwick Lane.

At last they stood before the College of Physicians. Tolly stared at the dirty windows and the quiet walls.

He felt Black Jack's hand on his shoulder. He looked up into the harsh face.

'If – if it's not what you hope . . . what then?'

'She'll not know. I'll never tell her!'

'She'll know, Tolly. Believe me, she'll know.'

'I'll make her believe me –'

'Then come away now. There's still time, let's not disturb it –'

'Are you afraid, Black Jack?'

'A little, Tolly,' murmured this huge man who'd lived through a hanging, broke open a madhouse and struggled to raise the dead. 'A little.'

'Oh, listen to the 'normous gent, young man!' moaned Mrs Gorgandy. 'Don't disturb what God and the physicians 'as laid to rest. Let sleeping secrets lie. Ignorance is 'appiness; I speak as a widder. Lord, young man, if you was to know a part of all the wickedness done in a single day, you'd not sleep of nights nor 'old up your 'ead for shame. Ignorance . . . blessed ignorance!'

'But there's always someone who knows,' muttered Tolly, his gentle heart moved profoundly by Mrs Gorgandy's words.

Black Jack's hand tightened on his shoulder.

'So you'll tell her . . . no matter what –'

Tolly nodded; and the fear left Black Jack's face. He mounted the steps to the door and began to knock and knock till the mansion shook under his blows. A frightened voice bade him hold his fire till the door was opened.

A porter peered out, and behind him appeared two aproned assistants.

'Mrs G! What's your business now? And at the front door!'

'Mr Mills! I ain't me own mistress – I'm 'ere by compulsion. They forced it out of me! They wants to view a Mr Carter of Reigate –'

'Mrs G! Names? You know better than that!'

Mrs Gorgandy looked abashed. Hurriedly she consulted a little black volume from her pocket.

'Number forty-three, Mr Mills. Begging your pardon – a squint at poor forty-three, if you'd be so kind?'

Now the aproned assistants took a hand. Forty-three was months ago. They were in the eighties, now. What was asked was impossible. But –

But what? Quick! Time was short!

But the Register might be of help. More than the eye could see was written in the Register. Not only outward circumstance, but all inward condition, such as only God could have known in life ... now revealed to the eye of the physician – after death. Would they care to see the Register?

'Fetch it!'

The huge Register, bound like a Bible and inked like a lease, was fetched and opened under the porch lantern. Its pages were turned, till –

'Number forty-three. Well-nourished male. Aged three and sixty. Was this your gentleman? In fine health, it seems. Might have survived ten years more. Nothing amiss anywhere ... save for the passage of a pistol ball through his heart.'

'Was it ... was it by his own hand? Can you tell – even now?'

'By his own hand? He'd have needed a long arm on it, young man. Though the ball passed clean through him, the breast wound was the greater, signifying that the ball was outward bound. I'm sorry to say that your gentleman had an enemy who proved mortal to him. Not to put too fine a point on it, he was shot in the back ... murdered, as we say –'

Black Jack stared. He grinned. He roared with laughter. He thumped Mrs Gorgandy on her tight shiny back. And Tolly kissed her.

'Who'd have thought,' roared Black Jack, 'that you'd have been some use to the world, you wonderful mint-new widder!'

19

HALF after seven, and the Town was on the move. Famous Mr Whitfield had been preaching in Hyde Park since six o'clock – a grave, fine, hopeful sermon fairly bursting its seams with salvation. Torch-led families streamed past Tyburn, flickering and murmuring and coming to rest in a quaking bulk about the inspired preacher. Far from the terror of gaping streets and crashing mansions, they crouched and strained on every religious word.

'Pills against the earthquake! Five shillings – who'll buy?' came the cry along Oxford Street as the man in the moleskin hat plied his extraordinary trade. But now he'd grown cautious and kept a sharp eye for the enormous monk and the hurrying boy who'd twice knocked him down. He watched out for them among the hastening, shadowy crowds, and presently moved southward, along Berwick Street, plucking at the skirts of another multitude, hurrying towards the river and the safety of ships . . .

'We'll lose them, Black Jack! They must be arrived –'

'Then up on my back, Tolly! One travels quicker than two on such a night!'

Now high above the dark multitude, Tolly swayed and rode the tide, bending low as they passed under overhanging shop signs, or as Black Jack staggered on uneven ground. Then their heads would be close together and Tolly would mutter: 'Hurry . . . hurry . . .' And Black Jack would nod till his sharp beard scraped Tolly's face and he'd bid him: 'Hold on, then. Here we go –'

And they went!

'Pills against the earthquake! Who'll buy?'
The cry was by the river now, moving towards Blackfriars.

The man in the moleskin hat dodged and darted shrewdly. He'd few boxes left – and little time. Either way – earthquake or nothing – his trade could scarce survive the night. So he'd come by great skill in avoiding upsets ... and applying the sharp elbow.

'Pills! Five shillings the box! Last orders, good people!'

No sign of the monk and the lad; but the man in the moleskin hat faced other problems. A youth in a baize apron, sharp-faced and with short, sturdy legs was plunging through the crowd regardless of obstruction. Angrily the pill-seller backed away towards the treacherous cobbles of Paul's Wharf ...

Hatch panted and groaned with extreme effort; but still he ran as if all the angels in Heaven were after him. The mad old man with the chopper! *He* was after him! Of this Hatch was utterly convinced. He was not given to fancies; never had been. Neither conscience nor remorse nor any other such feeble matter had driven him relentlessly through the frightened Town. Only the madman with the chopper. Sometimes Hatch heard him; sometimes – when he looked back – Hatch was sure he'd seen him. So Hatch continued to run, now with, now against the crowds that filled the streets. Yet he was always in full possession of his faculties. Neither the guilt of blackmail nor even the guilt of murder drove him on! These trifles were as nothing beside the terror of the madman's chopper. For it was here that Hatch had truly blundered. He'd waked an anger of huge proportion; a vengeance there was no placating.

'Earthquake pills! Damn you, you little madman!'

Exasperated beyond measure, the man in the moleskin hat jabbed with a shrewd elbow. At the same instant he put out a foot.

Hatch flew, danced wildly on the wharf's edge, then shrieked and fell.

The buildings, the shuffling crowd, the black wharf walls all rushed up to the dark sky as if in the grip of an enormous whirlwind. Then the troubled waters – in which were reflected the link-boys' torches – engulfed him like a freezing fiery furnace. There was a roaring in his ears, as of distant gunfire, till, like a chopper, came a violent blow to his head.

On the wharfside, the man in the moleskin hat peered angrily down as his last two boxes of pills danced in the wake of the waterman's boat that had just broken Hatch's head. Then he went his ways, while the crowd pushed and shuffled on, having missed entirely the earthquake, the whirlwind, and the ending of Hatch's world.

'Faster . . . faster, Black Jack!'
The huge man turned and stared up at the wild, impassioned face of the boy upon his back . . .
'Faster it is then . . .'
Onward he rushed, now along Tooley Street, now through Rotherhithe, scattering the multitude who still pressed on, out of the Town.

'Five pound for last places! Room for one more!' shouted watermen, whose craft were already filled to sinking. 'Come aboard before it's too late!'
They scraped and jostled in the lanterned river, till that last place was filled, when they'd heave out to midstream and pass on their trembling cargo to vessels of more consequence . . . and even dearer passage.
But there was one vessel which would have none of them. A very proper, neat and new-painted ship with Spanish work about the poop. Which Spanish work had been somewhat scraped and stove in by a waterman's pole.
'Keep off or I'll sink you!' came the stern cry whenever an overloaded boat drew near . . .

'Black Jack!'
The giant groaned. He was all but spent.
'I can't go no faster! I can't –'
'The wagon!'
Black Jack had lied. He could go faster. And he did. Like a

great dark wind he sped, with Tolly on his back. And as they ran, with the night air beating in their faces, Tolly shouted wildly and triumphantly, 'Belle! Belle! You're free!'

Then the people of Greenwich briefly forgot that only an hour of this last day remained in the wonder of seeing a huge monk with a ragged potboy on his back, plunge into a wagon that had been waiting at the river's edge.

An extraordinary wagon, lantern-lit from within, so that it winked and glimmered like an enormous painted lamp. It shook and rocked as if it were enjoying its own private earthquake; and sounds of unusual motions echoed from it along the wharf. Sounds of dancing feet – of laughter spaced with tears – of a girl crying 'Oh – oh,' as if she'd say more, much more, if only her lips would be freed for a moment ... Then came a sound of iron upon iron, as if a chain was, at long last, being filed through.

'Sheer off there – or you'll get this marlin spike through yer bottom!' a surly voice shouted down from the larboard side of the ship with the injured poop.

The small boat was dark – having no lantern. Four figures seemed to be in it, as nearly as could be made out; and they were calling up. But between the din on the river and the Captain's holding an Earthquake Service on the quarterdeck, the sailor could hear nothing plain. So he bawled again: 'Be off – or you're a goner!' and was satisfied to see the dark boat shift ... Out of the sailor's sight, the vagrant boat jigged and nudged under the dim light of *The Philosopher*'s poop lanterns. Which light revealed a sight that would have answered the surly sailor's worst suspicions. At the oars was ramshackle Jed, while in the stern, mountainous and wild, crouched Black Jack. His arms were enfolding a filthy potboy and a girl who looked for all the world as if she'd been newly wrenched from a madhouse. Not the boatload for *The Philosopher* ...

'That broken window yonder,' muttered Black Jack. 'I'll hoist you through.'

183

Some seven feet above them gaped the twisted golden mouth of a window the waterman's pole had gone into. Black Jack stood up and Jed steadied the boat against *The Philosopher*'s stern.

'She first –'

Belle offered her arms, but Black Jack took her by the waist and lifted her up into the night. As he did so, his leathery lips touched her cheek. He breathed softly in her ear.

'I will ... I will ...' she whispered; and then with a quick flurry of white ankles and ragged skirt, she was gone.

'Now you.' He turned to Tolly. 'D'you remember when I hoisted you through another window?'

'I've not forgot, Black Jack. Never.'

'Nor I – nor I.'

He bent down. The boat rocked violently. Jed grunted – then Tolly rose in the air. He came level with the window. Belle was waiting. She held out her arms as if to catch him as he clambered into *The Philosopher*'s Great Cabin. He looked back, and down to the man who stood swaying below him. The lanterns dimly lit the savage hills and valleys of his countenance which seemed like some fierce landscape in nature. Black Jack's eyes were bright ...

'God bless you, Tolly and Belle.'

'And you, sir –'

'Pull for the wharf, Jed! Pull quick and hard! Row, man – row till your back breaks and your heart bursts!'

Jed nodded and bent his back. The oars spiked the water and the boat began to move and nose its way rapidly among the craft that jambled and lilted the glinting river. White, uneasy faces turned to watch it pass – for it lumbered somewhat on account of the enormous gowned figure who stood and stared back to the neat ship with the Spanish poop. And from that same ship, first two, then one face watched and watched till the dark boat dwindled into the river's confusion, and Black Jack was become no more than a memory, printed deeply on Tolly's heart and soul.

'Stowaways! Scum of Greenwich!'

Mr Jarvis, *The Philosopher*'s mate, armed with cutlass and lantern, had heard noises and come into the Great Cabin. Outraged, he stared at what the wind had blown in. Objects such as even *The Philosopher*'s rats would have puked at. And how they stank!

'Mister Jarvis –'

Startled, the mate raised his lantern. And all but dropped it.

'My God! I think it's Master Bartholomew! *Is* it Master Bartholomew? No! Yes! It's him! My God – I'll fetch his uncle, the Captain! Stay there! Don't move! Your uncle, directly!'

He stumbled, staggered off – as if he was allowing for storm tiltage when there was none.

Belle grasped Tolly's hand. At last, his uncle, the sea-captain. All her mockery sank into uneasiness: even fear. Of what? The unknown master of her beloved Tolly's soul. The strong, shrewd, all-wise man whose spirit had overshadowed all of Tolly's life.

A clock in Greenwich had begun to strike. Then another seeming to answer. A curious silence crept over the river. Farther and farther away in the night, clocks banged and roared. The shuffling crowds halted. The multitudes about the churches and in the open spaces grew still. The clocks tolled on, counting out the end of April four.

Gentlemen in heavy riding cloaks, ladies in quilted gowns and even children, quite small, innocent children blanketed against the chill, looked up to the thick sky in which moon and stars were doused.

When would it fall – the wrathful Hand of the Almighty, bringing smoke, ruin and whirlwind to the poor, neglectful Town?

'Nephew! Bartholomew! Is it you?'

Who spoke? In the Great Cabin, Belle stared. She saw

185

nothing – her eyes being fixed fearfully on a space somewhat above the average height.

'Answer me, sir! Is it you?'

With a shock, Belle understood the voice to have come from a shade lower down.

Captain Dorking was not a big man. Belle bit on her lip. He was, to be honest, a somewhat small man, a trifle withered and wrinkled, like a nut. But he had a large nose and a chin that made every effort to rise and meet it. She bit on her lip more fiercely. She'd a strong desire to laugh...

The silent apprehensive multitudes were still waiting. Someone muttered that he fancied a sausage and a jar of mulled ale. Here and there began a shifting from foot to foot, and men began to eye the preachers with the beginnings of doubt. Where, oh, where was the vengeance of God?

In *The Philosopher*'s cabin, Captain Dorking was pacing peevishly to and fro. All thoughts of overhanging calamity were forgotten in his shock at his nephew's distressing state and wild companion. Was this the respectable, God-fearing, law-abiding country lad he'd honourably apprenticed to a draper? This – this muddy gaunt young man in a potboy's apron with a wispy, prettyish female in tow and in such rags as he'd not suffer to swab *The Philosopher*'s decks?

'For shame, nephew! For shame! And you a Dorking! Respectability – in tatters! Ain't there nothing left in your heart of all my careful teaching? Oh Bartholomew, you have disobliged me, sir! And be so good as to bid that female hold her merriment. I see no cause for laughter here!'

But there was no containing Belle. Not all her sense of fitness nor her strength of purpose could subdue the helpless laughter that kept rising within her. Her eyes overflowed, her shoulders shook...

'Belle!' muttered Tolly. 'My uncle – the – the sea-captain ...*Please!*'

'I'm s-sorry,' she whispered. 'But – but – oh Tolly, my love! He – he's such a *little* man! Such a ridiculous little man! And you – you, Tolly, are ... twice his size!'

Then to Captain Dorking's further anger and sense of being disobliged, his nephew, also, began to laugh ...

At half after twelve – which allowed handsomely for any discrepancy between the Town's clocks and those in Heaven, the multitudes began to look somewhat sheepish. Here and there, enterprising preachers offered that the Almighty had been prevailed upon by prayer to change His Mind. It was either that or all the Town's sins put together were of not much account and offended more against the Church than Heaven which seemed to be the more tolerant of the two.

At a quarter to one there was no more any doubt. Someone had blundered. The world had signally failed to go off with a bang.

But it was in Hanover Square – not in St George's, but in the middle of the square itself – that one Christian gentleman had the shrewdness to draw the only possible moral.

'My friends!' he shouted. 'Here's the Hand of God indeed! We're all alive! Ain't that the miracle? And the miracle of every blessed day?'

The Philosopher sailed on the morning tide. The window in the poop was boarded up – not so much against the weather as against any further nephews the Captain might have had. None the less, he was grown somewhat calmer. Mr Jarvis, being a family man, had prevailed upon him to consider that matters might have been worse.

'Worse, mister? How so?'

'The lad might have been dead, sir.'

'Aye. Indeed. That would have been worse.'

So Belle and Tolly were suffered to stay aboard and given the advantage of washing – from which they emerged creditably enough.

'He takes after me, eh, mister?'

'There's something about the eyes, sir ... and – and the set of the jaw –'

'And the lass ... neatly built, eh, mister?'

'Trim, sir; very trim.'

Now the breeze grew brisk; and under topsails and foresail, *The Philosopher* passed by Woolwich and spiked the rising sun upon her nodding bowsprit. She was bound for New England with cargo of broadcloth and muslins and fine brocades. A handsome vessel with twelve of her one-time thirty guns in good commission. Everything about her was brisk and neat and clean. Everything, save the ragged pair who stood upon the quarterdeck, and whose wild hair and tattered garments the breeze tugged at, stretching them out like the pennants of a hard-won victory.

Sea-birds wheeled and screamed about the foremast, and the sailors sang:

> 'So fair art thou, my bonny lass
> So deep in love am I –'

Then of a sudden, Belle whispered to Tolly – and his warm blood turned to ice.

'Do you see it? Do you see it, now?'

'What?' His fine strong world was suddenly adrift ... and falling. 'What?'

'A tall black tower with a golden top – higher than the sky. There are white angels flying with white wings ... and all the world's singing a lullaby, for the sun's gone to bed in a blanket.'

He closed his eyes in anguish. Once more, the insignia of her madness. The malady was returned.

'Do you see it, dear Tolly?'

'No – no – no!'

'Then open your eyes, Tolly! And look!'

He did so. Out of the darkness of her old malady, which was

gone forever, her vision stood at last in the brightness of day.

Like a tall black tower, tipped with the morning's gold, soared the mainmast – high in the realms of the wheeling white birds. While in the great canvas blanket of the foresail there nested the misty image of the sun. And Captain Dorking's sailors sang as always, liltingly:

> 'But I will never prove false to the bonny lass I love,
> Till the stars fall down from the sky.'

'Nor even then, Belle. Nor even then.'

Now Woolwich was left behind, and the ship coursed on down the river towards the wide dancing sea. Children waved as she passed and cried her, 'God speed.' And under her bowsprit, her learned figurehead seemed to nod an acknowledgement ... the wooden Philosopher whose features bore a striking resemblance to Tolly's uncle, the sea-captain ...

'God speed! God speed!'

'Indeed ... Indeed ...'

The End

Also by Leon Garfield

JOHN DIAMOND

Young William Jones discovers that his dying father is a swindler. When he sets out for London to right the wrongs his father has done to his old partner, Diamond, he finds the backstreets less than welcoming and all kinds of horrors lying in wait ... (Winner of the Whitbread Award).

DEVIL-IN-THE-FOG

An eighteenth-century story about fourteen-year-old George Treet who lives with a family of strolling players and is torn between pride in his profession as an actor and pride in the noble birth he is told is rightfully his.

JACK HOLBORN

A pirate adventure story in the best Stevenson tradition, bursting with fascinating characters and dominated by the figure of the mysterious captain.

SMITH

A twelve-year-old pickpocket is hounded through 18th-century London for a document he stole by accident.

THE SOUND OF COACHES

Sam Chichester grew up on the Flying Cradle, the coach that had been carrying his mother when he was born. She had died and the coachman and his wife had adopted Sam. But who was his real father?

THE STRANGE AFFAIR OF ADELAIDE HARRIS

Harris and his friend Bostock lose his baby sister, Adelaide, in an experiment. They search desperately to find her, but it looks as if she's gone for good, and in her place appears an unknown gipsy waif ...

MISTER CORBETT'S GHOST
AND OTHER STORIES

A chilling supernatural tale of an apprentice who wished his master dead – and got what he wanted. Also two other stories about a painter's assistant and a battle at sea, and a mutiny of convicts

THE APPRENTICES

'When I grow rich,' chimed the church bells – but for an apprentice in 18th-century London there was precious little chance he ever would. But he could hope, and dream, and the twelve apprentices whose longings are depicted in this dazzling story-cycle do just that.

THE GHOST DOWNSTAIRS

Mr Fast, the mean-spirited clerk, signed away seven years off the end of his life in return for the riches of the world, and never imagined the little lost spectre that could come to haunt him.

HEARD ABOUT THE PUFFIN CLUB?

... it's a way of finding out more about Puffin books and authors, of winning prizes (in competitions), sharing jokes, a secret code, and perhaps seeing your name in print! When you join you get a copy of our magazine, *Puffin Post*, sent to you four times a year, a badge and a membership book. For details of subscription and an application form, send a stamped addressed envelope to:

The Puffin Club Dept A
Penguin Books Limited
Bath Road
Harmondsworth
Middlesex UB7 ODA

and if you live in Australia, please write to:

The Australian Puffin Club
Penguin Books Australia Limited
P.O. Box 257
Ringwood
Victoria 3134